GUARDING MORGAN

Sanctuary, Book 1

RJ SCOTT

Love Lane Books

Copyright

Dedication

For JSC, whose help was invaluable with Joseph.
Any mistakes are mine.

And, always for my family.

GUARDING MORGAN

SANCTUARY #1

RJ SCOTT

Love Lane Books

Chapter One

"Twenty, one sixty-six, Altamont, western, black cat, lemon pie, twenty, one sixty-six, Altamont, western, black cat, lemon pie…" The words were on repeat in Morgan Drake's head, a litany, over and over, in case he forgot. His FBI shadow had drummed the words into him until he could repeat them in his sleep.

"Just in case, Morgan, okay? If there's any problem, you take these keys and the car I showed you in the next door basement parking, and you take Highway Twenty West onto the 166, head for Altamont, Western Street, find a bookshop called Black Cat Books. Someone will locate you there, and he'll have a password, okay? Lemon Pie. He's a guy I trust with my life, and his name is Nik. I'm writing his cell number on this paper. You need to memorize it in case I can't contact him. Can you repeat… twenty, one sixty-six, Altamont, western, black cat, lemon pie. After me…"

He lost the rhythm of the words as a dark sedan overtook him and then peeled away at high speed. Dread gripped him again and he fought hard not to hyperventilate. Taylor had told him this car would be safe in every sense of the word. Fueled, in good condition, and with plates linking to an elementary teacher in Queens. The convoluted route to the garage where the car was housed meant he would probably have not been followed. Probably. He couldn't stop the car. "Don't stop driving Morgan. Don't you stop for anything or anyone once you get on the road. Not FBI, not cops, no one." Taylor always finished his sentences with the simple question: "Do you understand?" No, Morgan didn't understand.

From the minute he had made the decision to be the designated driver for an after work party, everything had gone to hell. An hour of complete terror, in which his world was ripped apart, ended with him in an FBI safe house guarded by a gruff agent who played a mean hand of poker. Obsessive and compulsive about Morgan's safety, Taylor Mitchell, FBI, ruled the house with an iron fist, not letting Morgan slip into the role of victim for an instant. They talked about what could go wrong. Taylor gave Morgan worst case scenarios that literally blew his mind—shooting, mayhem, and possible death. Morgan wasn't sure his protector was supposed to do that. But he liked the guy and if a choice presented itself between Taylor and the other agent who split the shifts? He would take the warnings every time. Especially given the other guy had bad breath and a corny line in come-ons.

God.

Taylor and Morgan had only been talking before bed.

Morgan had been looking for the reassurances he remained safe, and Taylor had been only able to say he would do everything in his power to keep Morgan safe. Should anything happen, or go wrong, he knew of another man, another agency quite separate from the FBI, to help Morgan. A private agency called Sanctuary. Only brought in at the worst of times, it was there as an option if needed. A friend of his now worked for Sanctuary, an agency providing protection for people in need. Actually more than a friend. His ex-FBI partner. Morgan waved the information away, naively so it turned out later.

"How can anything go wrong? I'm with the FBI, the trial is in two weeks, and then everything will be normal again."

"Even the FBI can be compromised, Morgan. Don't you watch TV?" Taylor had a serious expression on his face. Now, with Taylor lying shot, and possibly dead, on the floor of the house, all Morgan could concentrate on was the list of directions he needed to remember, the promise of some mystical safety within his reach.

He waited for the sedan to make a U-turn and come at him with some bad guy hanging out of the window with a gun, but instead the indicators flashed and the car left the highway. Morgan's breathing stayed erratic and panicked sounding, despite how much he tried to settle it, fueled by the pain in his chest, his left arm, and his throbbing head. He didn't want to chance the radio. Music might help him find some composure, but shit, what if it meant he didn't remember the words in the right order? He'd probably end up in Canada or something, the bad guys chasing him down and taking him out of the equation in some blood and gore shootout.

Yes, Morgan watched the TV procedural cop shows with clever detectives or FBI suits who flouted the law and kept the little man on the street safe. He also saw the first witnesses in these shows were inevitably shot between the eyes, the last link in evidence on a high profile murder case. He'd also seen that sometimes the FBI agent was corrupt and a cop could end up on the wrong side of the law. He liked those shows. He simply didn't want to *be in* one of those shows.

"Twenty, one sixty-six, Altamont, western, black cat, lemon pie, twenty, one sixty-six, Altamont, western, black cat, lemon pie."

He struggled to keep from losing his shit and forced himself to unbend each finger of one hand away from the steering wheel. After he opened his window, the rush of cold early morning air cleared his eyes, and he breathed deeply, trying to gain control of his nerves. He checked the mirror. There was no one behind him; the road remained deserted, and he had a purpose.

Twenty, one sixty-six, Altamont, western, black cat, lemon pie...

Chapter Two

"FORTY-FOUR NINETY-FIVE," THE YOUNG GUY BEHIND the counter said with a wide yawn. Dressed in the red uniform of the gas station chain, he couldn't have been much past sixteen. Judging by the wide-eyed expression on his face when he looked up, post-yawn, to see his new customer, he either showed classic signs of being high or he was *really* shocked at Nik's appearance.

Nik tried not to laugh. Given what he'd seen of himself in the restroom mirror—blond hair flat, brown eyes dull and bloodshot and pale skin—Nik imagined it was probably the latter.

Three in the morning had closed in on Nikolai Valentinov far too fast, exhaustion stinging his eyes. Self-preservation prompted the stop at a gas station a short way off Highway 20. He probably looked like some kind of gun-wielding, staring-eyed, about-to-kill-everyone maniac. Add in the fact he was tall, built, and dressed in black from head to toe and he could appear menacing at all the wrong moments. Poor cashier-kid and his shit shift choice.

Placing the most reassuring smile he could muster on his face, Nik carefully counted out the cash for the charge, and they swapped the sum total of five words in exchanging money for gas, Pepsi and a Snickers.

He stopped for a moment outside the main door and glanced back briefly at the cashier who remained staring at him with a wide eyed expression. Then he stretched his arms high and breathed in deeply. Copious amounts of caffeine kept him going, but the down effects were hard to rein in, not the least of which was the two minute piss he had taken in the not quite so clean and ironically labeled rest stop. Any kind of rest in the filth littered on every available surface of the outside building was not an option.

Nik Valentinov may well have been way past simple tiredness, but even he had standards. Simply being weary had been pushed through on day three of his case, moving on to complete and utter exhaustion by day seven. Finally, this morning, his charge had given his evidence and had been rewarded, if that was the right word, with a place in witness relocation. Out of Nik's hands and hair, the witness was away from the auspices of the Sanctuary program and back into the system that only now had decided it would protect the witness.

Nik realized he hadn't moved from the spot where he'd stopped, and he had to admit, it made him more than merely a suspicious face. It made him a man who was simply plain odd, and a possible threat. Casually, he raised a hand in a small wave and finished the short distance to his car, stumbling over the island at the pump and finally, gratefully, leaning against the driver's door of his 4x4 and swallowing the first third of his Pepsi in seconds.

Nik could almost taste the downtime in his immediate future, three whole, *entire, complete* weeks away from close protection duty, from Sanctuary, from life. As much as he loved his job, the call of peace and isolation of his own place, with no high levels of alert and no college-aged hooker requiring his protection, called to him. Only him, and a beer or ten, and a good book, and *fuck*, at least one entire night of uninterrupted sleep, a rare commodity when on any case. He could function well with the benefits of small snatches of sleep until he let himself think "it's over", and then sleep was all he craved, all he needed. Another two hours and he would be home. Rolling his shoulders, he winced at the tightness in his neck and the familiar pain in his lower back and left knee. At this moment, standing here and looking up at the night sky, he felt every single one of his twenty-nine years, and then some.

Finishing off the Snickers bar in four bites, he aimed the wrapper for the wide open bin, missed by a good two inches, and then stooped to pick it up. He placed it in by hand, sighing at his complete lack of coordination. *I shouldn't be driving; this is stupid.* He was a danger to himself, and he wasn't entirely sure he would last the two hours left to home. The insistent lure of flashing neon across the highway called to him and the small no-tell motel offered a bed. Maybe not a fully clean bed, but hell, he had slept in worse. Maybe he should break this journey up. Resolving to do just that, he started the engine and yawned widely, feeling the crack in his jawbone. The ringing tone of his private cell didn't register as any kind of noise he recognized straight away. It just buzzed away in his subconscious until he finally put two and two together. The sound echoed low and he had to root for the source of the clatter in his laptop case. When he was on a job, his private cell stayed that way, private. To hear it sound still turned low reminded him he really needed to turn the damn thing up. Blinking at the screen, shock snapped him fully awake as he saw the name flashing there. He answered with a sense of urgency, thrown back three years to the working partnership he had invested so much into.

"Taylor?" He couldn't have stopped the alarm in his voice if he'd tried. The last time he'd heard from his ex-partner was over a year ago at his FBI debrief, a few weeks before he joined Sanctuary. To hear the man's voice now, a familiar southern drawl, twisted heavy, wet and rasping, sent concern skittering down his spine and chased exhaustion away in a rush of adrenaline.

"FBI safe house Albany compromised." Taylor's voice sounded more than wrong. Hearing the shakiness, the tone thick with pain, Nik didn't waste time on asking what had happened. Taylor didn't need to point out he needed help of some kind. Nik jumped into all business mode instantly.

"Talk," Nik snapped quickly. Training, instinct and friendship clicked instantly into place, and he focused every inch of his resources to listening.

"Shooter dead... mark gone to ground." Familiar words, and he knew exactly what he needed to say next.

"You tell them where?"

"Yeah. He knows. Can Sanctuary—"

"Me, not Sanctuary, I'm three hours out. I'll get him and make arrangements with Sanctuary. You're injured, call 911."

"On it." The call dropped, and Nik knew his friend would be contacting 911. Although injured, Taylor still appeared to be lucid enough to handle calling for medical help. Nik sent a quick thought of hope winging into the night and then snapped back to what he needed to do. He reached into the lock-box on the right of the dashboard. Fingerprint recognition released the security, and a small cover moved to reveal his work issued Glock G22. With practiced ease, he checked the chamber and slipped the loaded weapon into the shoulder holster under his black leather jacket. Taylor, plus an emergency call from a compromised FBI safe house, equaled a pressing need to be armed.

Lowering the driver window for the rush of cold air as he drove, he felt different as he left the gas station and turned back east on Highway 20. Gone was any idea of being off duty. He was focused, intent, and wide awake. Training kicked in immediately, and he was back in work mode. He assessed his location and what he knew, considering the information he had been given amounted to little. Not much to go on really, apart from his best friend and ex-FBI partner injured, a safe house compromised, and the shooter dead. The target Taylor had been protecting in the safe house had run. Who else was in the house? The feds would never leave just one guy with a witness. Was the other person dead? Maybe the witness had been injured. Would the witness himself actually listen to what Taylor had told him and try to find Nik?

Taylor had called *him* personally, instead of calling the safe house compromise in to FBI Operations. This meant one thing in Nik's mind. Inside job. Taylor clearly had a trust issue with handing knowledge elsewhere, especially internally. Unnecessary emotions flooded him, pushing aside the ice of his focus momentarily. Part of the job had to be to focus *on the job*, but shit, his gut churned, and he momentarily hoped to hell his best friend *had* phoned 911 straight after getting off the phone with him.

He wondered what kind of case his friend was on that he couldn't trust the FBI internally. Why hadn't he gone through official channels and approached Sanctuary? Why come to him direct? As newbie partners they had created a failsafe backup plan over beers and tacos just for this kind of situation. Only it had been in case either he or Taylor had been compromised, not a witness or someone involved in a case. Hell, it had started as a joke on a night out in a dingy bar. It was Taylor that started it; three sheets to the wind and in emotional mode. The beer took all his self-imposed barriers and kicked them to the curb.

"If something happens to me I want you to have my Spiderman comics," Taylor said seriously and downed the remainder of his beer in one gulp.

"Can I sell them?" Nik had replied. At that point he hadn't realized Taylor was actually being serious.

"Only if you promise to use the proceeds to spend the whole lot in a gay bar in one night."

"What is it with you and getting me to gay bars?" Nik had laughed, but Taylor had clearly crossed the bridge to utterly inebriated.

"Well, you won't get to fuck anyone here." Taylor looked over his shoulder at the significant number of couples weaving on the floor in an approximation of dancing.

"I'm not desperate, and I don't need to pick up a guy in a bar," Nik said in defense. He then proceeded to change the subject. "Anyway, if I die, you can have my gun." There. That should shut his friend up with the awkward shit.

"Your gun?" Taylor's eyes widened comically, and then he snorted beer in a bark of a laugh. "Fuck, Nik. Your gun! That is all kinds of serious."

"Ha freaking ha."

"What if we're not dead?" Taylor's words slurred, and he leaned in against Nik. Nik didn't move. To have his drunken best friend leaning all over him this way to Sunday was the only affection he allowed. He sometimes thought it would make his non-existent love life one hell of a whole lot better if Taylor was gay. At least Taylor understood the whole "serving the country and having no life" decision Nik had made. Taylor had made it too. Still, hooking up with a woman had to be easier than snagging a man. Especially for mostly in-the-closet Nik.

"What do you mean not dead?"

"Like, y'know, shot or something."

"Or something?"

"Yeah. We're separated, and you're shot, and we need a place to go."

"How shot am I?" Nik asked laughing, his smile widening when his friend's eyes crossed at the contemplation of how shot Nik would be.

"A through shot. Your arm maybe. Of course, you would be stoic and all Nik-like."

"Nik-like?" This was getting funnier by the minute.

"Yeah, all heroic and shit. Anyway, so you're being Nik, and you've been compomi—compro—compri —shit."

"Compromised?"

"Yeah. That one. You could call me and we'd have this place we could meet up." Nik climbed down off his stool carefully, ensuring Taylor didn't slide sideways to the floor.

"I need a piss, man. Can you sit up straight?" Taylor made a big deal out of slumping sideways to the bar, calling the bartender over and asking for paper and a pen. By the time Nik came back from maneuvering in and out of drunken half-dancing, half-staggering couples, Taylor had a somewhat lucid plan in place in half-legible writing.

"We always need a backup plan, bro," he had stated seriously, or as seriously as he could given the seventh beer pushing him way over the edge.

Nik had pulled the paper out the next day after he had watched, with some amusement, Taylor grasping the porcelain god in their shared bathroom. Written in stone was what they planned to do if things went south. Should a case go to shit as FBI partners, they had a place they would run to, a place to meet and regroup. When Taylor could finally see straight and stop being sick, they thrashed out the details. A single spot in the middle of nowhere had been chosen with a pin on a map and backed up with consideration for Taylor's taste in good pie. This was between them, no one else would know where it was. Passwords and verbal codes were agreed upon, and it had kept them both alive on more than one occasion. They didn't always work cases together when in the FBI. Then Nik had been injured, not the through-shot Taylor had foretold but much worse. A shot carved into Nik's knee and forced early retirement from the FBI and his days as Taylor's partner were over.

Nik had left without ceremony, joined the Sanctuary organization and, for one reason or another, hadn't seen Taylor since. Not in the last year, when all they had managed was a few coded emails here and there.

He had immediately keyed the place he and Taylor had chosen into his security coded navigation system. Black Cat Books, a book store and coffee shop on Western Street in Altamont. A small, fairly insignificant town based on size, it was only half an hour in distance but more than fifty years in atmosphere from Albany, then a few more hours to New York itself. It didn't seem like a place people assigned special meaning to, apart, he guessed, from the people who lived there. The bookshop was the focus of the community. It was a large open warehouse type affair, with coffee shop and meeting room and a state-sponsored library to the rear. This was exactly where Taylor's runner would have been told to go. Nik only hoped the witness had listened to what Taylor had said.

He had keyed the zip code into the navigation system, although he didn't really need it for direction. He used it more for time. The sparse night time traffic and a rush of adrenaline allowed him to drive without killing himself, and meant he would make it there around six. He settled into the rhythm of the road, connecting a call to Sanctuary and nodding to himself when the call was answered on the first ring.

"Enterprise Transports."

"I need to report an issue with a consignment in New York." There was a brief pause as a minute change in the air passed between them carrying the words, and then acknowledged confirmation of identity.

"Go ahead." The voice came across the air clear, concise, firm.

"Taylor called in a runner." There would be no need to explain who Taylor was. His new employers, a year of cases now, had a profile on everyone in Nik's life. Sanctuary certainly gave the impression they knew everything.

"Do you have a location?"

"Albany. The FBI safe house has been compromised. Taylor's down." Another pause and he heard tapping against a keyboard. The operator at Sanctuary understood he would want to know the situation with his ex-partner and was taking the time to check.

"It's already been called in, paramedics in attendance." Nik let out a breath he didn't even realize he had been holding. At least Taylor had managed to get help.

"Nik..." The voice changed slightly in tone, from all business to concern. "You're down for three weeks off-grid post-case. I can't allocate you. I need to get someone else to go in."

"No. I'm dealing with it." He didn't allow one drop of hesitation to show in his voice. His best friend had asked for his help, and by his standards, there could be no compromise. He wouldn't allow another Sanctuary agent to take the case.

"Noted," the operator confirmed. Nik imagined the woman on the end of the line shaking her head in exasperation. Sanctuary Operations, or Ops as they were normally called, were used to what they called "the idiot heroes" who worked for the foundation, with their I'm-dying-but-it's-okay bravado and weird codes of conduct. He couldn't tell one operator from the next, especially with the recording echo on the cell line. Although he had exchanged a few words with more than a few different operators in the office, he wasn't here to shoot the breeze or engage in polite conversation. He was all about cutting to the chase.

"I need to know what's open for me."

"Sanctuary Seven is empty. I'll send the GPS coordinates to your nav. Do you have an ETA?" Nik checked the screen and the new data that had been downloaded for S7. He added up the journey from here to Altamont, and then on to the general location of Sanctuary Seven, high in the Adirondacks, way past what people considered civilization. Every operative had a 4x4 as it was the only way to get to ninety percent of Sanctuary safe houses and he was convinced he would need it today imagining the type of accomadation there would be in the mountains. "Mid afternoon."

"Today?" The ops voice held no surprise. Sanctuary employees were used to working around tight deadlines.

"Today."

"Stay in touch, Nikolai. Don't go off grid without letting us know."

He didn't answer. He wasn't going to promise anything he might not intend to be held to. He didn't know what he would find in Altamont. He pushed the speed far enough to make a difference but just below being pulled over. Who would he find at the bookshop? His entire focus on this case, Nik Valentinov was on the clock.

Chapter Three

HIS HEART BEATING LOUDLY IN HIS CHEST AND HIS
fingers cramping on the steering wheel, Morgan finally
reached the turn to Altamont. Less than half an hour
remained before the dawn would fully push back the
night and he was scared to death of what daylight might
bring. His brain worked overtime on what had happened
in the safe house. The hail of bullets and the shouts for
him to run were a chaotic blend of explosive noise and
images. Was Taylor okay? He liked the agent with his
ability to talk and cover the otherwise awkward silences
as Morgan tried to think what to say. In their talks Taylor
had said if the house had been compromised then
Morgan shouldn't contact anyone. No using cell phones
and no land lines, where a call could be traced, no
visiting friends, or looking up family. He should go
straight to another safe place.

Taylor said there would be help there, someone who
could make a difference in this and keep him safe. He
left the main highway and headed directly into the town

where that safety awaited. Not for the first time Morgan thought he should never have said he would testify. He should have just run that night and kept on running. Why did he decide it was a good move to do the right thing?

He focused on street names down the long straight road until at last Western Avenue was the next left. He flipped the turn signal and followed the street until he saw the sign for Black Cat Books. He didn't know what he had been expecting, but this large structure wasn't it. Still, it must be what he needed to look for because it had the right name. Morgan pulled into the parking area and reversed into a corner space, with a wall behind him and the empty parking lot in front of him. He wanted to see anyone who could be approaching. A quick glance at the clock revealed the time to be half past five, and he waited and watched, not knowing what to expect.

The pain in his arm started to increase as the concentration he had needed to drive diminished. Knowing he had to check the damage, Morgan attempted to pull his black jacket to one side. He winced at the action as the discomfort turned to a burning pain, and he quickly released the pull on the sleeve. Blood had stuck the material to skin. There was a lot of blood. Most had dried, and while some of it showed wet scarlet, he guessed the cloth had done its job and stopped the majority of the bleeding. The burn of a bullet as it grazed his arm was a pain he didn't imagine he would forget in a hurry, but at least it had only winged him and not left him a gibbering mess on the floor. Thanks to Taylor, who had pushed him to one side in a dramatic ninja-type dive Morgan hadn't thought actually physically possible.

His protector had dropped the assailant with a bullet between the eyes and taken a bullet to the chest in the process.

He spared a thought for Taylor. He liked Taylor, quite apart from the man's prophesies of doom about the safe house being compromised and fleecing him of his last sixty dollars and ninety cents in poker. Taylor Mitchell was a good man, a good agent, solid, trustworthy, a coverer of all eventualities, dire or otherwise. Gorgeous as well, and hopelessly heterosexual—a real shame, especially given Morgan had spent most of day one in the safe house wondering if this whole protector thing would lead to bodyguard-type sex. Which it didn't. Clearly life didn't follow the scripts of Hollywood films.

Damn. Focusing on rambling thoughts like this didn't help his current predicament. The burning in his upper arm freaking hurt. He attempted to wipe off some of the crusted blood on his wrist where it had escaped his thin summer jacket.

Some time into Morgan's vigil, a person he assumed to be the owner or maybe just the manager of the early shift, opened the café and flooded the place with lights. Six am approached with a rush, and the parking lot went from empty to half full in a matter of minutes. Businessmen in suits rushed in and then equally as fast hastened out clutching coffee. Laborers in denim and t-shirts lingered in the café before leaving in groups of three or four. There were even a few cops who sat at the counter shooting the breeze. Morgan could see everything inside, the coffee and the breakfasts, and his stomach reminded him his last meal had been nearly twelve hours ago. The imagined smell of coffee lingered in his mind. He would kill for food or even just a black coffee. Shit. Bad wording.

A large beaten up 4x4 pulled into the parking area, and instead of joining the main line of cars, it moved to the back of the lot, as hidden in early morning shadows as he was. Could this be the person who had been sent here to help him? Or could it be someone who knew he was here and wanted to kill him? Morgan slumped into his seat, only peeking enough to watch as a large man— god, tall, way tall and broad—left the cab and stood for a moment. The guy was braced for action, feet apart, casually looking around the parking area, hesitating briefly on Morgan's car and then carrying on with the observation of other vehicles. Morgan couldn't see detail in the blurry, shady, early morning light other than the man's height. But the new guy seemed like what he expected in an off-the-records guy who would be his new protector. He wished there and then Taylor had handed over more description than just tall, broad, and blond. The stranger stretched and did a three-sixty of the parking lot one last time. He finally entered the cafe, haloed by the light spilling from the open door and was quickly swallowed by the interior as the door shut behind him.

Morgan waited ten minutes. His sense of self-preservation wanted the cops he had seen gone. If, as Taylor had warned, rogue FBI agents were responsible for an attempt on his life, then how the hell could he trust beat cops? How could he trust anyone? He didn't feel safe with cops there, and since the fateful night when the shit had hit the fan, he couldn't see a uniform without shuddering in fear. They finally left as the clock in his car nudged six-thirty. The patrol car peeled out of the parking lot, disappearing the way Morgan had come in. The cops hadn't given his car a second glance, so he guessed no bulletin, or whatever it was called, had been issued on his license plate or that the late model Toyota stuck out as being unusual. Taylor had assured him it was a clean car, and no one would know whom it belonged to since it was registered to some untraceable source. Even so, Morgan counted to ten after the taillights of the cop car had disappeared before he considered leaving his own car, his hands shaking as he removed the key from the ignition.

The quality of the light had changed with morning, brighter, but not enough, he thought, to reveal much sign of his mostly hidden injury. His dark jacket concealed the actual wound, and any blood had been camouflaged by the black material. He pushed his hands into his pockets as the attempts to clean the blood from his hands with the dry cloth he had found in the car had been a futile exercise. He needed a bathroom stop before anyone got a good look at him and his wound. He hoped to god the bathrooms were between the door and the café and he could visit them first.

He entered the coffee shop, expecting everyone to turn around and stare at him, or at least the one guy who would be expecting him. No one did, so he guessed his protector hadn't even arrived yet. Going straight to the bathroom, he emptied his bladder and stood at the sinks, hesitating to look at his reflection in the mirror for fear of what he would see. Maybe he should attempt to remove his jacket and clean the wound, but a closer look under flickering strip light showed it would be a really bad idea. No fresh blood showed, and the material really had formed a protective cover for his torn flesh. Best left alone for now, despite the pain knifing into him every so often. His hands as clean as he could get them, Morgan shook the dizziness from his head and moved out into the well-lit café. Shoulders back, he inhaled deeply and crossed to the counter, which was a large and clean space. There were cakes and pies under glass coverings, and the scent of coffee hung heavy in the air. The café itself flowed seamlessly into a large second hand bookstore—a cavern of titles and rows of books, piles he itched to dive into and look through. Reading? Shit, like he had the inclination to read—it had been the old Morgan who relaxed with a beer and book. The new Morgan had a death threat hanging over him and a head full of images he wished he didn't have. Sighing, he glanced around at the people drinking and eating, wondering who the hell among the customers sitting there would be taking the next step with him in this whole nightmare.

He ordered coffee—black, no sugar—and a slice of apple pie and then chose the table in the very corner with his back to the wall and his eyes on the room. Terrified didn't even begin to describe howhe felt or the anxiety and fear that curled in his stomach. From this vantage, he could see all the occupants, including the guy who had walked from the 4x4, three tables of laborers whose voices resonated in the high-ceilinged room, and the group of women chattering over coffees and fruit plates. There were a couple of tables with single occupants. One with the man he had seen, another with a businessman reading a newspaper, and, at the last one, a woman on her own, touching up her makeup using a striped yellow and pink vanity case. Without making it obvious, he observed each in turn, but instinct had him focusing on the man from the 4x4 as much as he could, simply because it seemed like he was the best option among the other guys at the tables around him. He racked his brains. Taylor hadn't mentioned anything about this Nik guy, what he really looked like, nothing except tall and blond. Tall was a given, and he had judged height when the guy had stepped out of his 4x4. His blond hair proved to be more of a light brown under the bright lights. Long and unkempt, it clearly struggled to hold a style and was a few weeks past needing a haircut. Stubble darkened the tall guy's face, and he had an air of a tired man on a long journey. No one except Morgan seemed to be giving the strong guy another look. Dispassionately, Morgan observed the black leather jacket and the navy t-shirt stretched across a wide chest and a face holding an expression of serious thought. One hell of a gorgeous man, he was equally quite a scary looking man. Rumpled, exhausted, hard—all words Morgan could think of to ascribe to him.

Maybe he was checking in with Taylor. Maybe he had called the cops. Maybe—shit—he was employed by the Bullen family and had somehow tracked Morgan here to kill him. For all Morgan knew, the guy sat there playing Scrabble, but he sure did seem very serious with whatever held his attention. No one else at the six or so tables looked to be of any interest. Nor did a single person appear remotely interested in him. With a sigh, he cupped his mug with both hands, briefly bent his head closer to it, and inhaled the fragrance of fresh-brewed coffee. Taylor had promised he would be safe here, and no one other than this nebulous protector Taylor had promised him would have any idea who Morgan was. Bullen wouldn't—couldn't—have tracked him down this fast.

"Hey," a voice growled, deep, a rough gravel of sounds, and Morgan nearly spilled his coffee in surprise, not sure how he had slipped from hyper-aware to barely awake and nodding off in his drink. He looked up, startled, as the tower of man from the other table slid in opposite him, placing his mug and pastry in front of him. Fear shot through Morgan, and he tried to stand. He felt the need to run, but couldn't coordinate the rise. The physical paralysis was terrifying, but the other guy didn't appear to have a gun in his hand or any other means of dispatching Morgan Drake from this world. For his part, the other man just stared at Morgan steadily, his brown eyes expressionless. The waitress chose that particular moment to drop off Morgan's choice of pie, and then sashayed away with a tuneless whistle, apparently oblivious to the petrified Morgan in his about-to-die standoff.

"What?" he managed to blurt out in an extraordinary push of something less than coherent.

"It's good." The other guy indicated the plate in front of Morgan. "But you should try the lemon pie."

Morgan looked down at his pie and then back up at the tall guy, seeing he had extended his hand in greeting. Lemon pie? The code word. This man he had been checking out, dangerously gorgeous, across the café was Nik? He supposed it made sense, but his height and breadth were as far from the smaller blond Taylor as could physically be possible. A mountain of a man, he looked like he had been dragged through a hedge backwards. All stubble and scruff, close up he certainly didn't look like any suit-wearing bodyguard Morgan had ever seen on TV. Where was the tie for a start? Cautiously, Morgan took the hand, wincing at a strong grip and then felt disconcerted as the new guy leaned forward, still hanging on to Morgan's hand.

"Taylor told me you would be here." Not only did the guy with the cow-brown eyes, the long lashes, and the broad chest start talking to him, but he used Taylor's name. Taylor. Wait, Taylor.

"Do you know…? Is he… alive, okay?" The whole sentence had started as a valid question, but it tumbled unconnected and rambling from Morgan's lips before he could stop it. Tall and hulking didn't comment at the way Morgan tripped over his words, but he nodded.

"I had a sit rep. He called 911." Sit rep? Morgan's head felt muddled, his ability to understand drifting away by the minute. Wait. Situation report. *Aaaah*, he got that one, and thank god it seemed Taylor was at least in safe hands and not bleeding out on the carpeted floor. "Nikolai Valentinov." The words flowed into one, but even though the syllables appeared European, the accent held all New York City vowels.

"What?" Morgan had tried to structure a more cohesive response than earlier, but apart from voicing concern for Taylor, the single word formed all he could muster from his confusion and shock.

"I know it's a mouthful, Russian heritage believe it or not," the bodyguard said ruefully. "Call me Nikolai, or Nik." Finally *Nik* released his grip, and Morgan quickly pulled his hand back, flexing and tensing it and then hiding it in his lap.

"Morgan. Morgan Drake," Morgan replied quickly and quietly. Bodyguard, no, *Nik*, nodded in understanding.

"Finish your coffee, Morgan. We need to hit the road A-sap."

Morgan swallowed a large mouthful in an effort to get some caffeine into him before Nik wanted them to leave, the heat burning a trail down his throat. He spluttered at the instant pain. "Where are you taking me?" he managed to push out, finishing with a cough. Nik shook his head as he threw bills on the table to cover the charge. Clearly Nik wasn't into sharing the whole "rescue Morgan plan" with the victim. He should have guessed he would get an enigmatic answer.

"Somewhere you'll be safe."

Chapter Four

MORGAN WAITED BY THE CAFÉ EXIT, OBSERVING NIK AS he rested his elbows on the counter and conversed with the woman working there. Young, built, and blonde, she leaned back towards Nik, blatant flirting apparent in every angle of her body, and they exchanged a few words, spoken low and intimate. When he finally left the blonde and joined Morgan, he simply smiled and opened the door, gesturing for Morgan to follow. Despite wanting to, it wasn't as if he could ask Nik how well he knew the woman. Anyway, why this question even formed in his mind he didn't know. He had more important things to worry about, more relevant questions to ask.

"Where *exactly* are we going?" The question was a valid one, and asking a second time was certainly done in the hope he would actually get an answer less cryptic than "somewhere safe". Nik looked at him quickly and then turned his attention back to the 4x4, popping the locks and opening the passenger door.

"Inside." Clearly this was all Morgan could expect to receive in answer for now, and he quickly scrambled into the seat, pulling the belt and securing it, only wincing slightly when Nik shut the door firmly. When Nik finally climbed in and started the engine, Morgan realized the other car remained, the little Toyota that had borne him away from danger and into Nik's protection.

"What about my car?"

"It'll be collected." Evidently Nik was a man of few words.

"And our destination?" One last poke.

"Sanctuary Seven in the Adirondacks."

"In the mountains?" He couldn't stop surprise from coloring his voice. He had never been far out of the city. New York born and Albany bred, he was a city boy to the core. The country and the mountains held fears for Morgan that were almost, but not quite, on a par with the homicidal maniac who wanted him dead. And hang on, what was Sanctuary Seven?

"More in the wilderness."

The wilderness? Great.

"What is Sanctuary Seven? How do I—"

"Morgan," Nik interrupted with a wave of one hand, turning the wheel and peeling out of the parking lot, "right now, shut up so I can concentrate." Morgan did exactly what he was told, not wanting to jeopardize anything keeping him safe.

Five minutes into the journey, Nik pulled the truck to the side behind a stand of trees and bumped up on to the rough grass area to the right. He stopped the truck and turned in his seat.

"Do you have a cell on you?"

"Taylor told me I shouldn't have a cell. They took mine when I went into the safe house." He realized he'd rambled when a simple yes or no would have sufficed. "No. I don't have—"

"Are you wearing jewelry, a watch, have any hidden piercings?" The words were staccato short and interrupted Morgan's rambling effectively.

"No." Morgan was confused. "Why?"

"I need to check if anyone has a way of tracking you. A tracker could be hidden anywhere."

Morgan looked down at himself, eyes zeroing in on the belt in his jeans, the only metal he had on him. Or anything remotely stable enough to hide a bug. His t-shirt had no buttons and his jacket was thin and a zip up. Shit. A zipper? "My belt or the zipper?" He thought he could probably be coming across as ninety-five percent stupid, but Nik didn't laugh at him. He simply leaned over and examined both. What if there was something sewn into the material of his T?

"This belt was yours when you went into protection? And the jacket? Have either been away from your sight at the safe house?"

"Yeah, all my clothes were—"

"Get out of the car," Nik ordered and reached into the glove compartment, pulling out a scanner wand similar to what Morgan had seen at concerts when they randomly checked for knives and such. Morgan didn't fight the barked order, climbing out of the cab and assuming the standing position with his legs spread for Nik to carry out the scan.

"Is there anything?" he asked to break the intensity in Nik's expression.

"No."

Well, a brief and really to the point answer is better than no answer at all.

When Morgan was deemed clear, the two men climbed back in the cab and continued with the journey. A couple of times Morgan opened his mouth to talk but realized he couldn't think of anything vitally important to talk about if it meant interrupting Nik. Anyhow, Nik wasn't exactly the most talkative of saviors, and Morgan subsided into contemplative silence. About an hour into the journey he wanted to ask if Nik had any pain pills, but it didn't strike him the large man in the seat next to him would be the type to resort to pills. Probably not even for a bullet wound or a broken leg. The thought made him smile inwardly, and it occurred to him for the first time since last night he felt safe. It formed a very nice feeling.

Looking out of the side window, he watched Altamont disappear in the side mirror, and as they rejoined the main road then merged back on Highway 20, he became lost again in his own thoughts. He wished he could hold on to that feeling of being safe, but he had too much in his head to process, and before long, a maelstrom of messy fear and anxiety churned in his chest, and he couldn't relax.

He had never considered himself strong. He hated confrontation, and he guessed others labeled him as a quiet, unassuming man. People saw what he tried hard to be, a friendly guy who bent over backwards to accommodate others, not stepping on toes, not causing trouble. The sum of that resulted in a good path in life and one that had, until recently, worked well. He had a good and stable job in admin for a credit card company. Not a job to set the world on fire, but it paid enough for his small one bedroom apartment and a limited social life. He had friends at work, other cubicle workers he spent lunch time with. He went to parties here and there. For some time the year before, he had even had a boyfriend for a whole twenty-three days. With his high school education and lack of college degree, it was the most he could probably hope for to be happy and mostly settled.

Right up until his "of course I can" accommodating nature left him designated driver for an office night out and put him in the path of a killer. He wondered if his fellow cubicle rats missed him, or even wondered where he had disappeared to. He hadn't been back to work in three months, nor had he returned to his apartment. He probably had been missed. After all, he did all the coffee runs. He bet his team members were all suffering horribly from caffeine withdrawal. He shuddered. A whole team of six being so miserable from lack of coffee was not a pretty sight.

He shifted in his seat, allowing more of his weight to lean against the door, the seatbelt cutting into his neck. The pain in his left arm increased, and he wondered if maybe the damage would prove so extensive it would disable him permanently. He didn't even want to think about further damaging his arm. How would he be able to sketch? He was left-handed, and his hobby of capturing his perception of life about him in art and cartoons was important to him.

"Satellite sweep?" Nik's voice startled Morgan from his black thoughts, and he turned instinctively towards Nik. He opened his mouth to ask him to repeat the question and then almost as quickly realized Nik was talking into a hands-free headset. Morgan listened to the one-sided conversation, a chill of apprehension skittering down his spine as each word defined Nik and who he was at this moment in time. "We're clear. Do we know if he's still alive? ... No, it's not something I want to contemplate... Is Seven checking out?"

Seven. This would be the Seven Nik spoke of before, Sanctuary Seven, and the questions tripped to the tip of his tongue as to what the hell Sanctuary Seven actually was. He guessed it was a place. A house. Maybe a cabin if it was high in the Adirondacks.

"Run a check for me... I know... seven four one seven Alpha Iota Delta." Nik paused, tapping his fingers on the steering wheel, and then continued. "Send it to my cell. K-five. Do me a favor. Pass on the sit rep to Taylor and tell him to stay the fuck away. His boy is a ten. I put him at a Cat One." Nik glanced at Morgan then, a thoughtful expression on his face, and Morgan looked back at him steadily. What the hell made a Cat One? And why was he a ten? "I know Taylor well, warn him about tails and tell him to stay in the hospital." Nik ended the call abruptly, clearly having covered what he needed in a jumble of sentences and codes.

"Is Taylor still okay?" Morgan finally dared to ask. Nik cast him a considering look.

"It'll take more than a round to the chest to get rid of Taylor," he stated simply with no ceremony. That had formed the longest sentence Morgan had heard from Nik. Then a question came from him that near knocked Morgan from his seat. "How are you holding up?"

"Me?" *I'm fucked, tired, petrified; my stomach is in knots and my arm? Well, my arm hurts like hell, and I feel like death warmed over.* What if he said all this to Nik? Would it interrupt Nik's concentration? Take his eyes off the ball? Instead, he just said, "Sore, but I'll be fine." *It hurts like a bitch.*

"Stopping to check you out isn't my priority."

"Okay, that's—"

"If you need medical attention, I'll give it to you at S-seven." The words were calm and efficient, and at that moment, Morgan could believe Nik was some kind of superman able to perform major surgery he sounded so confident.

"Thanks."

No more words in response to that one. Nik undoubtedly wasn't ready to share the other half of the phone conversation, and Morgan couldn't make much sense of only Nik's side. The last thing he wanted was for Nik to be distracted from either driving or remembering numbers so Morgan stopped his careful observation of the sexy man in the driver's seat and leaned back against the window. He closed his eyes against the dizzying blur of the blacktop beneath them. Nik wasn't driving particularly fast, but the constant *clack clack clack* of tires on road joins and the *whoosh* of the cab passing trees as they entered a more heavily forested area proved enough to lull him into a semi-doze.

"Morgan!"

Morgan blinked awake, sickness rising from the pit of his stomach at the interrupted nap, and attempted to push himself upright.

"What?" he managed. Nik slid him a quick look, redolent of something Morgan identified immediately as criticism. He shuffled in his seat, berating himself for shutting his eyes and for causing the man looking after him to be dissatisfied. Leave it to him to fuck up.

"We're going off road." Morgan looked around him, at the sun that broke through the canopy of the trees every so often and at the dense undergrowth that curled around and about each trunk. He couldn't see a road diverting from the main one.

"Okay," he finally offered, pulling his belt tighter around him and grabbing the handle of the door as the front wheels hit dirt and potholes. Turned out a road did shoot off the main one, but to call it an actual *road* was being very generous and probably an affront to blacktop everywhere. More of a trail, at some parts, it wasn't even wide enough to avoid the bushes and plants that grabbed greedily at the 4x4's paintwork. For every hole, there were three more of them. For every stomach churning dip, there would be an ear-popping climb, and before long, the twists and turns had him completely disorientated and turned around. He thought the main road lay behind them, but it could have been to the left, or the right, or god, he didn't know.

The pain in his arm had worsened, and the nebulous

sickness in him was becoming more of a reality. He was utterly convinced the bleeding had started again as the bumping and twisting carried on for way too long. Nik didn't look much more comfortable. His knuckles were white on the steering wheel, and he wore a strong expression of determination on his face. Morgan didn't want to interrupt the man or take his own focus away from not jostling his arm any more than he needed to. Morgan attempted not to stare, but failed miserably. Staring at dangerous, scary Nik was infinitely better than knowing where the next pothole would be.

They turned off again, this time onto what could euphemistically be called a wide footpath. Suddenly Nik pulled sharply right then left and stopped the engine. This was good as Morgan really thought he might well lose the entire slice of pie he had eaten at the café. Not to mention nearly passing out with pain from his wound.

Nik left the cab almost immediately, pulling a weapon out from under his jacket where a holster clearly sat. He jumped down into what looked like a tangle of undergrowth and then fought his way around to Morgan's side, cursing loud enough for Morgan to hear. Finally he had Morgan's door open, holding back foliage with his body, and he gestured to Morgan to climb down. Morgan gripped tightly on to Nik's hand to get out of the cab, but he released his grip as soon as he could. He wasn't some girl who needed help, and he didn't want Nik thinking he was.

"I haven't been to Seven before," Nik stated, indicating the forest closed in around them. "It's fucking tight."

"Tight?"

"Dense, deep, hidden, off the beaten track."

"Oh." Morgan could have smacked himself as he trailed after Nik through plants and weeds as tall as his groin. "Oh" wasn't a particularly clever bit of conversation. To be fair to though, pain stole his breath, and he didn't have brain capacity to waste. Sighing inwardly, he concentrated on Nik's denim-clad rear, watching muscles bunch and contract as the stronger, taller man carved a way through the bushes until finally they entered a clearing and the tangled edge of a thin ribbon of water.

"The truck will be hidden from sight," Nik supplied helpfully, and then gestured for Morgan to stay where he was.

Weapon at chest level, Nik approached the building in front of them and began a sweep of the area. Morgan had grown used to the whole jumping-about-checking-things business from his time with Taylor. That wasn't what had him staring with his mouth open. No, it was something very different that made him stand in utter bewilderment.

A structure. It was the kindest description his brain could think of. It certainly wasn't a house, or a functional cabin, or anything in between. Four decaying clapboard walls melded with the trees. Long sides made of timber were the same color as the trees, green and covered in growth, and some at crazy angles. True, it was probably nicely camouflaged, but it was difficult to see the elements of what could be considered decent housing in the tumbled mix of wood.

Nik returned, holstering his weapon and then rolling his shoulders.

"It's clear," Nik announced.

Of course it's clear; it's a fucking shack in the middle of nowhere. No self-respecting assassin would wait there for me. Jeez, where did *that* little hissy fit come from? Thank god he hadn't actually verbalized it or he'd have come across like some kind of drama queen.

"It looks kind of..." Morgan wondered how he could word this diplomatically, "... old."

"Oh," Nik responded carefully, and then nodded. "I've seen worse on the books."

"Worse than this?" Morgan allowed his horror to seep into his voice. This special agency Sanctuary had safe houses worse than decaying timbers wedged into a forest? Worry washed over him at the thought. He was in the middle of nowhere, halfway up a mountain in an environment alien to him. Could this Nik guy actually protect him? Doubts built on exhaustion, pain, and his less than stellar reaction to the decrepit structure in front of him. What if someone found them? If it turned out to be a federal agent who had revealed the location of the first safe house, then surely one dilapidated cabin in the middle of nowhere wasn't the best place to stay. How could it be guarded? Where were bars on the windows? Come to think of it, where were the freaking windows?

Nik chose to ignore the comment. "Come on, kid, inside there'll be coffee." Morgan's ears pricked even in his despair and pain, and he chose to ignore being called a kid. He was twenty-four, not eighteen. Pain killers and coffee would be a definite tick in the plus column, even if the coffee had to be made over an open fire in a tin can. Then the doubts crept back in. What if there was no wood for a fire? One solution would be to burn a wall or something. Oh god, what if there were no way of making a fire? He didn't know how to start a fire, and he wondered whether or not superhero Nik knew how. He followed Nik up to steps, which didn't look like they would hold the weight of a squirrel let alone a fully grown man. Nik jumped them in one go, the porch not, in fact, collapsing under him, and Morgan gingerly took one big stride over the three death traps masquerading as steps, jarring his bad arm as he steadied himself on loose railings. The stride took him straight up behind Nik, so close they were touching, and Morgan stumbled back to stop himself from collapsing into the bodyguard who didn't appeared perturbed at the action. He simply looked back at him and raised an eyebrow. Talk about if looks could kill.

The door was plain enough—*it has a door*—and unyielding, more so than the fragile looking walls around it, and carefully Morgan touched the aged wood. It didn't feel right, didn't have the rough texture he'd expected. It sure looked like wood, but it felt warm to touch and solid.

"It's not wood, is it?" he commented softly.

"The outside is a cover for the structure inside." Nik stated this so damn simply, like it would be obvious to all but the most stupid. Morgan didn't know whether to feel stupid, angry, or just to sit on the floor and cry.

"Oh." Now Morgan didn't know what to expect, and

eagerness spiked in him, so much so he wished he felt strong enough to push past Nik in his enthusiasm to see what the inside was like. He flexed his arm experimentally, bile rising in him at the pain, and supported it with his other hand. There would be no pushing to get in front just yet. He stepped inside after Nik, blinking at the change from daylight to near dark.

What little light there was sparked on chrome appliances and windows with glass in them and— "Holy shit," he stuttered in disbelief, "it's a freaking secret Bat Cave."

Nik closed the door behind them, leaning back against the entrance and watching him.

"So it's a house inside a shack?"

Nik shrugged and moved to the small kitchen at the back of what appeared to be a main room. Morgan took a few moments to look closer at what constituted his home for the foreseeable future. Flagstones lay with a haphazard pattern on the floor, and there was decent furniture as well as a flat-screen TV on the wall and... cushions. There were freaking cushions. How was it possible the outside looked so rough yet this structure was so sound? Couldn't people find this? Walkers? Hikers? So many questions churned in his head. This new protector was clearly an expert in both monosyllabic responses and not actually talking at all, much like Taylor, because he said nothing to expand on the house inside a house idea. Nik opened a small dropdown flap high on the wall and pressed a sequence of buttons. Soft light illuminated the inside. Morgan wanted to check out the rest of the place, but equally, he wanted to sit before he fell down.

"What if someone… found this and d-decided to live here?" There was a definite stutter in his words, and it was getting worse. His head knew what it wanted to say, but his body was letting him down. He gritted his teeth against their chattering and the sensation like cotton wool in his mouth.

"No questions. Your arm needs attention. Bathroom, now."

Strident and forceful, Nik's voice came from right behind him, and Morgan jerked back, pain radiating from his wound. Plainly this new protector of his had some freaky ninja skills in creeping around quietly. Morgan followed him to the simple bathroom holding a walk-in shower, a toilet and a sink. The shower looked good, big enough to stretch tall. God, what he wouldn't give for a shower.

"We'll need to get your shirt off," Nik said, opening an under-sink cupboard and pulling out a box labeled with a big cross to indicate medical supplies.

Throughout his flight, Morgan had been conscious of the bullet's damage, but the shirt had formed an effective plaster, soaking enough blood and then forming a bandage against further bleeding. If Nik removed the fabric, shit, the possibility of worse pain hit him.

"Do we have to?" Dizziness assailed him, and he closed his eyes briefly.

Nik ignored the question. "Take the jacket off, strip, all apart from the shirt, and then stand in the shower for a bit to soften the fabric enough to remove it from the wound." Another long sentence but one tinged with a special kind of impatience. What Morgan said next came out of his mouth with absolutely zero conscious thought, the only thing guiding him his normally flirtatious nature and the high degree of pain. Well, that was his excuse, and he was sticking to it.

"You just wa-want me wet and ha-half naked." He stumbled over the words and then could have bitten his tongue off immediately. Lowering his gaze, he shuffled back to the bed. This would be the point where he either got a fist to the gut or had to explain himself.

Nik snorted in response and then gave a sharp, "Just get in the damn shower." Nik actually attempted to assist Morgan in removing the jacket, but a stubbornness he didn't know he could be capable of forced Morgan to take a single step backwards and away from Nik's touch. Nik would probably just rip the damn thing off and claim it easier that way. Morgan paused in removing his jeans, glancing over at Nik who was staring in a completely different direction.

Morgan wondered what was wrong with him. Why was he refusing help when the taciturn ninja offered it? And why the hell did he suddenly feel so damn shy? Jeez, he'd stripped in front of Taylor all the time, like brothers or best friends. Until of course the other fed in charge of his protection took too much of an interest in what he felt Morgan had to offer. Morgan didn't usually worry about stripping in front of other men, and he certainly wasn't ashamed of his body. In fact, he worked hard to keep his high school swimmer's body in shape. At twenty-four he still had a flat stomach, and while not overly muscled, he was a fit guy. Okay, at the moment, he was only semi-conscious and his thoughts weren't making sense, but other than that, he was fit.

"Supplies," Nik announced and excused himself at the same time, and Morgan waited until Nik moved way out of the bathroom before he kicked off boots, toed off socks, and pushed down jeans one handed, all the time leaning against the wall. When he pushed away from the wall, he registered blood there. His blood. Dizziness washed over him, and he was exhausted and hurt. Sleep was all he wanted and needed. Step one in the list of barriers to him getting sleep was the shower, and determinedly, he stepped inside. Whatever the cabin lacked in looks, it certainly didn't appear to lack hot water.

The sudden sensation of warmth on his skin caused him to feel sick, and he gagged into the stream. He wasn't actually sick, but he knew that was only because his stomach had run on empty. Determined, before he fainted like a girl, he managed to slip off as much of the shirt as he could until, supported with his hand, the only part of the shirt that still touched skin was the encrusted sleeve. Blood ran in trails of pink, diluted stains tracking a path to the drain where it swirled down to wherever water went in the middle of nowhere. It was too painful to allow the stream to impact directly on the carving in his arm, and he angled himself so the mist worked its magic without touching the actual injury. The material eased slowly, and the quality of pain changed from sickness to focused hurt.

"Okay?" Nik's raised voice startled him, but to his

credit, the man hadn't actually come into the bathroom. Warily, Morgan eased the material away from the wound, a little piece at a time, wincing at the pulling on newly formed scabs. What he uncovered looked red and raw and bloody, not good at all, but it wasn't the end of the world. Hell, at least he was alive. He turned off the water.

He drew in a deep breath. "Out in one," he managed to force out, his teeth chattering again, and he dropped the shirt into the sink. Finally he pulled a robe from a hook and draped it over his shoulders, grateful for the warmth. He then wrapped a towel around his waist in at least some form of modesty. Steeling himself for what he knew had to happen next, he stepped into the bedroom. Nik had his back to him and stood gazing out of the window at the tangle of trees beyond the glass. Clearly hearing Morgan come into the room, Nik turned, and for a second, they were frozen in a tableau. Morgan might have been wrong, but for a second, he thought he saw unabashed and instant appreciation in Nik's face. Seriously, he needed to cut out all this damned wishful thinking. What the fuck was in his head to make him think this over six feet of built guy was gay, let alone interested in a pathetic wounded feeling-sorry-for-himself witness?

"I… um… managed to get the… um… thing off." Lucidity went out of the window, and he shrugged at his inability to explain, cursing the instinctive movement as his skin pulled the wound.

Nik immediately moved to his side, examining the injury with the careful competency of experience. Within five minutes, maybe ten, the wound was cleaned, dressed, and a bandage placed over it.

"It's more burn than wound," Nik offered succinctly. He yawned widely, stretching, rolling his broad shoulders, and then cracking his neck. He looked exhausted and probably needed sleep. It was daylight outside, and Morgan realized this would be hour twenty or so without sleep for himself.

"Do you have the time on you?" he asked, warmth seeping into his body as he gingerly dried himself as best he could with another towel. "I don't have a watch. It got left at… it got left." He'd inherited the watch from his granddad, and it had been left on the nightstand at the first safe house. He didn't want to think about never getting it back.

"A little after two. Sleep now, questions later."

"I think my arm is too… sore… to let me sleep," he admitted.

Nik pointed to water, pain killers, and a steaming cup of hot chocolate in front of him. "Meds for you, and a drink. The meds are kind of strong, so they'll help you sleep." Morgan picked up the tablets and swallowed them with a mouthful of cold water.

Nik knocked back his own drink, and Morgan wondered if the man had cast iron for a mouth and throat, because he himself still blew on his.

"Morgan, I need a code." Nik suddenly asked.

Morgan blinked and shook himself into the present. Nik had asked him for a code. What code?

"I don't have a code."

"No, we're setting a code for you. Do you have a memorable string of numbers? It's for lockdown."

"Lockdown..." What the hell? "Ummm... sixteen, three, four... one six three four." Sixteen years old, three dates to wait, then four orgasms in one evening. Certainly memorable.

"Okay, look, if you are inside and you need to secure yourself then there are keypads spread around the structure. Like this." Nik keyed in the pattern, and the effect was immediate. From seeming open and a bit shaky, the structure simply shut down. Bars appeared across windows, doors snapped shut, the echo of locks closing off rooms sounded, and suddenly, the air held an oppressive feel. Morgan's half-full mug dropped to the floor.

"What the fuck?" Suddenly he was back in the alley behind his apartment block, his friends all safe at home and his bed little more than a few seconds away. Then he saw it. A man with a gun at some girl's head, then nothing, as flight pushed him to run. The sound of the gun and the dead girl all blurred into the need to escape. He felt the shaking, only half understanding it was Nik who was holding him and saying something. Shit, shit...

"Are you with me? Shit. Only in emergencies. Morgan... are you with me? I've released the locks and doors." Half stumbling with Nik holding him, Morgan slumped to the floor and then lay flat on his back, his eyes screwed shut. He settled his breathing, shame flooding through him. He'd thought he had a handle on these panic attacks now.

"I didn't mean to scare you." Nik's gruff voice

betrayed some of his emotion, and the normally confident take-charge man showed a level of concern that stilled Morgan's fears.

"Sorry." He wasn't completely sure what else to say. Stupid idiot, getting all worked up over some freaking doors.

"'S okay. First time I saw lockdown it freaked me out as well."

Shit, I bet you didn't panic like a girl.

Nik said, "We both need sleep."

Helping Morgan to stand, Nik proceeded to show him three bedrooms. None of them were overly big, but each contained a double bed, an attached cubicle with toilet and sink, and a closet. And inside each closet, as Nik showed him, was a selection of clothes. Nothing too stylish or trendy, but sensible serviceable pants and fairly unisex t-shirts in different sizes.

The slightly larger of the three rooms also had a cot wedged in the corner, and Morgan didn't even want to think about a family being in a situation where hiding was the only way to keep them alive.

"Which room would you like?" The question echoed in his head, and irritably, Morgan attempted to string together a complete sentence, but the pain and the journey and the medication and the fear of death all made him one thing. Sleepy. Instead, he shrugged and just walked into the first room, crossed to the bed, and still in his towel and robe, he lay down. It wasn't the room with the cot, Jeez, it was obscene to imagine a child as scared as he was at this moment in time.

"This one," he said, and then closed his eyes. Nik would look after him.

For a good while, Morgan didn't move. Sleep was elusive, and he decided to just lie as still as he could. He heard lockdown again. He hadn't even realized Nik had reversed the shut down while he was freaking out, but clearly he had. The windows were barred, and the doors locked. The meds really kicked in, and his arm no longer throbbed like a bitch. He thought, running through everything that had happened to get him here, in a dark room, in a dark house, in a dark, dark forest.

He snorted at the turn of his thoughts, quoting the kids' books he loved. He might only be alive a little while longer. Unless of course Nik could do his job and become his knight in shining armor. Questions tumbled and twisted in his head, the buzzing stopping him from sleeping. Who had made the beds for them? Who put clothes here and medical supplies? Why didn't hikers find this place and sleep here?

God, these meds are good. I need sleep.

Clumsily, he pulled the quilt up one handed and around him, careful to lie on his good side. Feeling safer than he had in a long time, he allowed sleep to pull him under, images of Nik in his head.

Chapter Five

ACROSS THE SMALL HALL, NIK FOUND IT HARDER TO LET sleep chase him down. In effect, he had worked his way past total exhaustion and his body and brain had evidently settled now on an adrenaline-fueled alertness he couldn't shake.

Sanctuary Ops had confirmed the case had been passed on to them. Morgan William Drake, cubicle worker, wannabe artist, twenty-four, single, was now a Sanctuary Foundation concern. The dead shooter at the feds' safe house had been identified as one Filipe Ensiro, a gun for hire, no trace of money to him. Every suspicion pointed to the same person currently incarcerated for the contract murder Morgan had witnessed. How he had managed to arrange anything from inside prison was beyond everyone at the moment, but the general feeling was there was another person involved in the whole mess. The feds suspected an internal FBI leak. Ops couldn't comment on the theory as

they had no access to the more detailed FBI evidence.
Yet.

This was Nik's sixth witness protection case with
Sanctuary in the twelve months he had been with them,
but it would be the first time he found himself this
unprepared. He verged on panicked about how little
information he had. Sanctuary always passed a case to a
protector with every little piece of evidence collected by
the cops or the feds. This time, though, there hadn't been
a chance to give Nik any kind of heads up. All he knew
was Morgan had witnessed something important and was
therefore a Category One risk.

Nik didn't know enough. He hadn't had the chance to
read through case files in detail, and for a few brief
moments, he considered heading to the upstairs office
and going through the whole thing step by step.
Protectors needed intel, and he was freaking naked
without it.

Morgan had been a man in the wrong place at the
wrong time, and Nik hadn't lost all of his compassion in his
work. Not only that, but Morgan was one nice-looking and
intelligent guy. He clearly looked after himself and had set
off Nik's gaydar like *whooooah*, especially after Morgan
had thrown the comment at him before his shower. One
simple insinuation Nik wanted him wet and half naked and
Nik had lost his cloak of invincibility and his focus on risk
assessment and planning. Added to that, Nik's libido had
reasserted itself in the bedroom when Morgan had come
out of the shower with only a towel around his waist and a
robe precariously perched on his shoulders. It was far too

dangerous to have anything akin to attraction on a case, but the shorter man ticked all of Nik's boxes—dark hair, blue eyes, tight ass, strong, muscled but lithe body. The wound on Morgan's arm had seen a lot of consistent but slow bleeding, stopping when the shirt soaked up the blood. It was too late for stitches, but he made a mental note to suggest to Morgan that, when this was over, he might want to consider getting plastics advice.

Wait. Where the hell did that thought come from?

The comment about Nik seeing him wet and naked had slipped effortlessly from Morgan's mouth in a flirty manner. Morgan had immediately regretted saying it, which was obvious, because his shoulders had stiffened and he'd looked embarrassed. Stupid really, because if Morgan could read Nik's mind, he would see exactly what Nik would like to do to a wet, naked Morgan under completely different circumstances. As it was, he was a witness, under his protection, and in pain from a bullet wound. Nik's dick made a halfhearted attempt to be interested in getting off to the thought of a wet, naked Morgan, but his body and his mind betrayed his libido. Instead, he ran through a checklist in his mind, focusing on surveillance, intelligence, and what the hell he was going to do if he didn't get some damn sleep. He was on the edge and really needed downtime.

His thoughts didn't last long because a wide yawn cracked his jaw, and sleep became the priority. Information or not, a tired operative was a dead operative. He began to run through the usual things to help him sleep, stretching and then relaxing every limb in turn, and finally the sleep he needed so badly began to creep up on him. He turned onto his stomach, the reassurance of his Glock under his pillow, and thought briefly of his new charge in the half-world before sleep.

This wasn't the time for any sexual thoughts pertaining to Morgan. It actually wasn't the time to wonder about anything. Now was the time to sleep.

———

MORGAN WOKE DISORIENTATED and in pain and gratefully swallowed more pills left by his bedside. It was still light outside, but that meant nothing. It could be the same day; it could be the next day. He needed some way to tell the time and the date before he went mad from lack of information. Without a frame of reference to time, he instead listened to what his body told him. He recalled being woken when it was dark outside to be given meds. So that meant this must be the next day. He pulled on blue sweats and a pale blue t-shirt, and blinking the tiredness from his eyes, he left the room.

He had the chance to explore the structure he was relying on to protect him. The bedroom he had chosen as his own overlooked the mountain as it dipped and curved gracefully to the distance. He decided inventory would be good and rooted around the bathroom. Supplies were not short filled. There were about ten kinds of shower gel, shampoos, razors, condoms, and wedged in the back of the deep undersink cupboard was a small box marked with a red cross. Curious, he pulled it out, pressing the catch to open it, wondering if it was just a smaller version of the box Nik had used last night.

Opening it revealed boxes of pain killers, bandages, a thermometer, kids' Tylenol, and a multitude of other things, including more condoms. *What was it with the condoms everywhere?*

He found blankets, underwear, stuffed toys and even a box of LEGOs. He sorted through it, pulling out instructions to build some kind of train station. Wow, did that bring back memories of childhood.

A casual investigation didn't turn up any sign of Nik.

"Nik?" Morgan called the name and he heard a faint reply, noticing another door from the main living area. The steps behind the door led up to a fourth room under the roof, built into what could loosely be described as an attic, with a desk, computers, and lock boxes to one side.

"Morning," Nik offered from his seated position.

"Is it tomorrow?" Morgan asked carefully. He was aware it sounded like one hell of a stupid question, but hopefully Nik would know what he meant.

"It is. You slept a good fourteen or fifteen hours."

"Thank you for bringing in pain killers in the night."

Nik didn't answer, simply nodded his response, and Morgan moved to look out of the small window.

He could see the stream he had spotted on arrival, and the way it widened out into a larger body of water. It was edged with a forest that didn't give much quarter for any kind of reasonable shore line.

"Lake Dante," Nik offered, and Morgan turned back to face him. Nik was frowning down at his cell. "Apparently it stretches quite a long way through the forest." Curious, Morgan leaned over to look at the tiny map on the cell. There was nothing in any great detail there. Nothing but green and the small body of water.

"I should imagine it's left from the glacier," Morgan began conversationally, then before Nik could question what he was saying, and before he revealed how much of a geek he was, he looked back out of the window spotting a path to the water and a broken tangle of wood. "You think that's some kind of jetty?"

Nik joined him at the window. "Maybe. I don't know how old this place is, or even how long Sanctuary has had it."

"See, you said it again."

"Said what?"

"Sanctuary. Like it isn't something you find to keep you safe, like a church or something, but like it's an actual thing."

"It's a thing. Did Taylor not explain?"

"All Taylor said was, and I quote, 'twenty, one sixty-six, Altamont, western, black cat, lemon pie'." Nik huffed a quick laugh, and Morgan had the warm and fuzzy feeling he got when he said something that made people smile.

"Let me check in with Ops, get some food in us, and I'll give you the whole spiel."

"'Kay." Morgan leaned against the wall, looking at the edges of the lake, watching two stunningly marked kingfishers fly and dive and bicker, fascinated with the graceful ballet they performed. He half listened to Nik, who was typing and talking at the same time. There were more code words and half finished sentences but not one mention of his name, the guy he'd witnessed killing that girl, or even the Bullen family. His thoughts drifted over the last few weeks of all he had seen and all he would have to do, but he didn't get far into the thinking when Nik interrupted his thoughts.

"I need to show you the code system again. Can you handle it or do you want to wait?" Morgan realized Nik was talking to him. Something about the alarm system. Trepidation clutched at his throat, and he coughed so he could talk.

"I'm fine." Surely what happened last time had been an aberration. After all, Nik had locked them in when Morgan was half asleep the day before and he hadn't panicked then. They went downstairs to the kitchen, and Nik demonstrated lockdown using the code Morgan had offered up.

Being half asleep had clearly softened the edges of panic because the anxiety twisting inside him was visceral in daylight. This time when the lockdown happened, Nik released the doors and Morgan managed to scramble out of the front entrance. He crouched in the small tangled yard breathing mountain air and was close to full-on hyperventilating. Nik said nothing. He simply followed him outside and then offered a hand to help Morgan stand. Gripping Nik's hand, Morgan clambered to his feet, trying not to wince too much at the sharp pain in his upper arm. He finished upright and close to Nik, still holding him with an iron grip. The feel of the other man was like soft over steel. He was so built, his shirt stretched over his broad chest, and at this moment, he looked at Morgan with something in his brown eyes akin to concern. Coughing again, this time to cover his embarrassment, Morgan let go of his hold and took a step back, his heel squashing something in the undergrowth. Pushing down the need to see exactly what he had trodden on, because it was probably something high on the yuck scale, he surreptitiously wiped his boot on the grass and walked back up the steps to the front door, Nik at his side.

"I would apologize," Nik began, "but I think we need to try lockdown again and see if you can handle it."

"What if it takes all day?" Great, he just sounded whiny.

"We have two weeks until you are due to give evidence." Nik wasn't being funny. He was being deadly serious, and Morgan stifled the panic and the feeling of lightheadedness from hyperventilating.

"Does this place come with beer?" he asked quickly. Alcohol might help with the being-locked-in problem.

"Several types."

"Beer would be good."

Chapter Six

LATER, AFTER SIX LOCKDOWNS AND FINALLY A SEVENTH where Morgan didn't lose his shit, Nik stood in the kitchen and pulled together an omelet and toast. Okay, it was made with powdered eggs, with rehydrated mushroom and onion, but it tasted as good as it could.

As they ate the omelet and drank the frankly awesome coffee, Morgan decided he was going to launch into question mode. Nik groaned inwardly.

"Food, coffee, clothes," Morgan began. "How do they get everything here? What about milk and fresh stuff?"

"There's always a second way, sometimes a third, to every Sanctuary safe house. We can go and find it tomorrow; it's best you know where it is."

"So someone came in here, when? Yesterday before we got here? Or is it always ready?"

"Ops would have organized it all." He scrubbed a hand over his stubble. "This job isn't the first to come in unexpectedly."

"You said before you'd tell me about Sanctuary in more detail."

"You want to take this into the other room?" Nik suggested, grabbing his coffee and leading the way. *Might as well get this over and done with.*

"Sanctuary is funded, owned, and run by Jake Callahan. He was like me, an ex-fed, but from money; his family had *obscene* amounts of money, actually. Still, he put his life into the work, and you wouldn't know he wasn't like the rest of us. He was retired with disability from the FBI in his late twenties, but he couldn't let go. Setting up this network of places, where people go when the system can't keep them safe, was what defined him."

"So this Jake guy set up Sanctuary with all of his own money?" How much money would that take?

"Totally. It's a self-funded foundation, and Jake called it what it is, a Sanctuary, somewhere safe. The authorities know it's there, and they make use of it if they need to, but it has total autonomy."

"How many safe houses are there?

"I don't know entirely. A lot, more than fifty from what I see of other cases."

"So you haven't seen them all?"

"Nah, I work mainly out of the Washington DC area. I've only seen three of the houses."

"Are they all like this?" Morgan waved his hand. "Run down on the outside and high tech shit on the inside?"

"There's a standard for interiors in them all. I know that much, but I haven't seen specs on every one of them.

Some are suburban houses, some in the middle of nowhere, some in high-rises."

"They're not all remote like this one?"

"Not always. Others are secure apartments in different cities or towns. I do know every one of them is high tech."

"Can you tell me something about my case?"

"I can try."

"Why would Taylor not just call for FBI backup? Why did he send me to you, to Sanctuary? Why would he get you involved?"

"There's only one reason he would want you to go to Sanctuary—if he felt the feds couldn't protect you anymore. He believes strongly in the FBI and the job they do, believes they are the first and last line of defense, but for him to call me, he must think there's some serious internal problems to not trust his own people." Nik paused, tapping the fingers of one hand on the arm of the chair. "I read more of your case when you were asleep, and the cop they arrested for the murder isn't saying anything, not giving any names."

Morgan nodded, tilting his beer bottle and watching the contents touch the top on one side. "He won't tell anyone why he killed her. There has got to be a reason why a cop is willing to go to prison with his secrets."

"The usual I guess, money, or fear. I know they are looking at his family, at whatever coercion is being used to keep him quiet." They sat in companionable silence for a short while until it almost seemed as if Morgan had run out of questions.

Then he started on something way more personal.

"What was your last case, then?" Morgan asked, filling the silence in the room. And wasn't that opening a can of worms.

"A guy, seventeen and a male prostitute."

"Seventeen, jeez." Morgan sounded shocked.

"I've seen younger and a lot worse."

"Why was he in your protection? Did he see something? Do something?"

"Parties he attended gave him access to things best left hidden and ended with him witnessing rape and murder at one of those parties."

Jeez. That world was so far apart from his own. Despite that he was now in the same boat as Nik's last charge.

"And he testified?"

"He did."

"Kinda brave, I guess," Morgan said thoughtfully. "Why did *you* and Sanctuary get it then, if it was murder-related? Why not a safe house of some kind with the cops or FBI?"

"Long story."

"We have two weeks," Morgan said, echoing Nik's statement from earlier.

It hadn't been a particularly high profile case to start. It had been handed directly to Sanctuary when the witness wasn't deemed enough of an asset to garner full FBI protection. It didn't seem to matter the kid's testimony was enough to remove at least five or six medium-level dealers. If the FBI was after higher, then that's where their resources went. It angered Nik now as it had when he was still a fed. Placing an inherent value on the life of a witness because of who they could lead to, or what quality of crime they had been involved with, was wrong. It meant, more than likely, it would be that particular witness who became a casualty of war and conveniently "disappeared" during long drawn out cases. Hence Sanctuary, and Nik, stepping in where they could.

"Since we have two weeks, we have time," Morgan pointed out again, and damn it, if it didn't make Nik smile.

"He wasn't considered a strong enough asset to assign protection to. Sanctuary gets notified when the feds or the cops cut someone loose. We try not to turn anyone away."

"Was it a long case?"

"Twenty-two days." Twenty-two days of angst and crying and screaming and shouting, and laughing…

"I guess you got to know the guy pretty well then?"

"He was a nice kid under the grime of the crime, so to speak, but he was an addict, swinging from high to low in a flash. Wanting safety and reassurance in one breath and needing a fix and his old life back in the next. He had a lot of problems, not least of which was his need to keep offering me sex as a way of showing gratitude." Morgan was nodding like he understood. How could he understand any of what Nik had been through over the last few weeks?

"You said no though," Morgan said.

"Of course I said no. I like my men—" He cut his words off abruptly, not ready to share that particular thought process with Morgan. "Look, it was intense. Twenty odd days of paranoia, laughter, tears, regret, sadness, hyper-happiness... you name it and every absolute place on the emotional spectrum was covered."

"Poor kid," Morgan murmured, and Nik felt irritation rise in him. *Poor kid?* It was mind-numbingly hard work, and Nik had averaged maybe two hours of real sleep at any time. How about poor Nik?

"It was a suicide watch, and it wasn't pretty," he pointed out roughly, convincingly cutting the conversation direction dead. He was furious with himself he had looked to Morgan for some sympathy for the three weeks of hell. He didn't need sympathy or understanding or for Morgan to look at him like he was some god damned hero.

"So I'm right... At least I think I'm right," he said, tripping over his words again. "You are gay, aren't you? Is that why you left the FBI?" Nik raised his eyebrows at the direct question. It wasn't a secret anymore. Sanctuary didn't give a shit who Nik slept with or where he found comfort, as long as he did his job. It wasn't about politics and sensitivity. It was about getting the job done with the minimum of fuss.

"No. I wasn't really out. They knew, but I never said outright, and I did my job. I was retired out of the FBI when I was shot on a case. The bullet shattered the top of my tibia and my patella in the left leg, I have metal plates there."

"Shit, they made you leave? Couldn't they give you desk work?"

"They didn't make me leave; they offered me a cubicle job. I declined. Who the fuck wants to stay in a cubicle all day?"

Morgan wrinkled his nose, and Nik recalled that was exactly what Morgan was. A desk jockey. He sighed inwardly. All of sudden he was worried about hurting Morgan's feelings? Jeez. That was new. *Change the subject. Change the subject.*

"I was approached by Taylor and Sanctuary, and I decided to move on."

"Oh." Morgan didn't ask why. He probably thought he had pushed it too far already.

"And yes, I am gay," Nik added on a yawn. "But no, it didn't affect my time as a fed, nor my friendship with Taylor."

"I'm gay," Morgan supplied helpfully.

"I know."

"Fuck." Morgan frowned and then shook his head. "Can I have no privacy? They have freakin' everything in those files of yours."

"Not in your files, idiot. I guessed you were when you suggested I would like to see you naked."

"You could never accuse me of being subtle," Morgan shrugged. They subsided into silence until finally Nik spoke.

"I need sleep. I know it's only six, but I really have so much sleep to catch up on." Nik yawned again as if to emphasize the point and then pushed himself to a stand. "I'm going to lock down. Okay?"

Morgan nodded, and Nik had to smile when to his credit, Morgan winced only slightly when the bars slid over the windows and the doors locked.

Chapter Seven

THE NOISE OF THE SATELLITE CELL PHONE WOKE NIK, and when he peered at the screen, he saw Operation's code flashing in white on black. Four in the morning. The world hated him. Cursing, he tried to hit the right button to answer, succeeding only in knocking the phone from the stand and onto the floor.

"Fuck." His expletive was more pathetic than forceful, and he managed to scrabble for the cell, connecting the call and falling back on the pillow.

"Nikolai, thought you'd want to know that Taylor is out of surgery and looking good." The words filtered through the sleep clouding his mind.

"Thanks." Taylor's progress couldn't be the only reason Ops had called. They didn't do extraneous matters in business time. There was obviously something else to be added.

"Dale got assigned to work the case." Simple words, but holding so much meaning. Dale was Nik's backup in cases where two Sanctuary operatives were needed. An ex-Navy SEAL, he was one of the best they had. "The breach in Morgan's security has definitely been identified as internal FBI."

He waited for Ops to say more, but the woman talking didn't add any details. She knew she had said enough to explain the situation. Nik shook his head to shake the last cobwebs, sitting up and swinging his legs so his feet were flat on the floor. He needed to concentrate here, and the cold against his bare soles certainly sent a shock of adrenaline through his body.

"Is there any compromise on our position?"

"Not that we can see from here. Looks to be a quiet two weeks for you."

"Can I get sit reps from Dale?"

"Already in the protocols. I've also uploaded some more information. Looks like the boy is clear in all of this." Ops didn't elaborate, but Nik smiled inwardly at calling Morgan a boy. The call ended, and suddenly, at ass o'clock in the morning, Nik was grasping a satellite phone that had gone quiet and he was completely and utterly wide awake.

When his head hit the pillow the previous evening he hadn't expected to sleep this long. There would be no way he would get back to sleep now, and he judged he had probably managed a good nine or so hours recharging, which was better than normal. He guessed now was as good a time as any to download some of the newest information and updates on Morgan, and after a quick shower, he sat down in the attic office and logged on to the Sanctuary server. He had full case operative access to the encrypted folder, which was named

#drake6012. With fresh coffee in hand, he started to skim the details.

The basics he already knew from his work yesterday, but it was reassuring his own research was backed up by hard facts. Morgan William Drake, twenty-four, worked in admin and was a wannabe artist. That much he knew from Ops' initial hand-over, but the rest was kind of new. No surviving family, his father died in 1996, his mother had been taken by cancer in 2003 and his step-dad killed in a car wreck in 2005. Morgan had a high school diploma and a clean record every parent would want for their son, all culminating in the nice safe desk job.

There were files and scans in a sub-directory labeled for the Bullen family. The details of the organized crime included politicians bought and paid for, prostitution, drugs, zoning issues. Thomas Bullen, patriarch of said family, had run for governor, interestingly financed by donation and what else? Drug money probably, thought Nik decisively. The feds had clearly been working on some kind of connection between organized crime and the family that allegedly held markers on most of the low lifes in Albany and had a reach stretching way over to New York City.

Something in all of this paperwork connected the Bullen family to the death that Morgan had witnessed of Elisabeth, or Beth, Costain. Twenty-eight, as her case sheet summarized, she had died in a dark alleyway behind Morgan's apartment. According to Morgan's eyewitness report, it was Gareth Headley, a cop with twenty-three years on the force, who had carried out the shooting. Nik read between the lines. It didn't explicitly say so, but the victim had connections, an ex-boyfriend that carried the surname of Bullen. Hell, you only run with the big guys in organized crime so long before you died or disappeared or were forced to hide. He opened a text screen and typed in a few connecting sentences, then sat back in his chair and studied for patterns in what he was writing. The one question bugging him was why the cop who carried out the shooting, this Headley, wasn't talking. What connection did he have to the Bullens? And if there was a connection, what was it the Bullens had on him to make this otherwise normal cop a killer?

"Hey." The voice startled him, and he spun in the seat, his eyes widening at Morgan standing in the doorway. His charge was sleep mussed and rubbing his eyes. He looked adorable, cute, warm, and the protective part of Nik just wanted to guide him back to bed and maybe climb in for a close cuddle. "What time is it?"

"Umm…" Nik pulled his thoughts together, realizing belatedly what was all over the screen behind him. He closed down some of the windows, pretending to look for the time. "Six-thirty."

"I couldn't sleep, saw the light, what ya doin' up?" Morgan asked and leaned against the door frame.

"Got a call about Taylor. He's out of surgery and looking good."

"He's a nice guy. I liked him. He didn't give me all the shit."

"Yeah, Taylor's a good person to have your back." Good. It was a safe subject to focus on. Less chance of focusing on the sight of Morgan's sleep pants tenting with his morning wood.

"How do you know him?"

"Partners in the FBI, before I left to join Sanctuary."

"The other agent, Oscar," Morgan began, "had bad breath and went from hating everything I stood for to wanting to get in my pants." He straightened from the door, straddling the spare chair and wheeling closer to the screen. Nik wondered how it was possible someone with hair sticking up in all directions could possibly look *that* hot this early in the morning. Close up, in the rarefied early light, he saw that Morgan's eyes were not simply a plain blue, but a mix of sapphire and flecks of jade green, with lashes that swept low with every blink. Pretty eyes, the color of the sea in the Caribbean.

"What do you mean?" Nik heard himself ask, forcing the lyrical thoughts from his head. It was important to diffuse these thoughts immediately before he compromised his professionalism.

"On the one hand, he said he would have no hesitation in shooting me if it turned out I had anything to do with shooting the woman in the alley. Or indeed if I had known anything about what was happening before that girl died. On the other hand, he propositioned me twice."

"Twice?"

"Well, when he found out which team I played for, it was placed to me in terms of 'we have time to kill, fancy sucking me off?', which I have got to say didn't work well. In fact, he spent the next hour bent over from where I kicked him in the balls."

"He's an asshole."

"Then when the first case evidence came in, and it

didn't clear any connection between me and the dead girl, things went from bad to worse. It was like I became less in the guy's eyes, a possible criminal. That just made him think he could force anything he wanted on me."

"Shit."

"Taylor stopped whatever it was Oscar the bad cop thought he would do at the business end of his gun. Like I said, a good man there."

Morgan placed his hands on the back of the seat and rested his chin on them, and Nik wanted to reach out and touch him, in reassurance he was more like Taylor and less like this Oscar. At the same time, embarrassment sheared through him. What the hell was he thinking even getting that personal? At this point, he was willing to bet some of it was the brain in his pants doing the deciding.

"You're checking my case file," Morgan observed. It wasn't a question, and there was a slight cooling in his voice.

"I need to get a good handle on everything that happened."

"Why? The case isn't anything to do with what you are doing for me. You just watch over me. You can't do anything else."

Nik folded his arms across his chest. "If I know why you are in protective custody, then I can make sure you get the right support. It may be you know things you didn't realize and you can talk to me."

"Talk?" Morgan closed his eyes and kept them tightly shut. "I don't need to talk anymore about it. It's all written down. There isn't any way talking is going to help. Unless you can scrub what I saw that night from my brain using only words."

Nik sat taller in the chair. Morgan's words dripped with sadness and darkness.

"Do you want to talk about what you saw?" he asked in his best talk-to-me tone. It wasn't as if he was trained in counseling, but he could pretend. Maybe lulling Morgan into feeling secure meant the other man would remember something he hadn't before.

A full body sigh shuddered through Morgan, and he opened his eyes, the pupils dilating in the light and so much hurt in their depths it carved a pain right through Nik. Morgan opened his mouth, as if to start talking then shut it again before pushing the chair back and standing. He stretched tall, his fingertips brushing the high ceiling, his shirt riding high and exposing a tantalizingly warm, toned strip of skin and the start of a dark enticing treasure trail. Nik swallowed. The sweats were riding low on Morgan's hips, and his hip bones were just there…

"All I want from you is to help me cover my bandage somehow so I can shower and then point me in the direction of some more awesome coffee," Morgan stated firmly, and with a nod, he spun on his heel and left the room, the noise on the stairs indicating he had left the attic area entirely.

So he didn't want to talk about the night it all happened. Nik could handle that. He'd have to dig for information in other ways. He would be there for the other man if he was needed. Protection was what he did best, and with a sigh, he trailed downstairs to the bathroom to help cover the bandages with plastic wrap and tape.

———

NIK SAT DOWN OPPOSITE MORGAN, both with coffee, and Morgan devouring toast. The kitchen was a wonderland of stainless steel, top-of-the-line appliances. On his hands and knees, Morgan had discovered a coffee maker in a bottom cupboard. Apparently his next mission was to find the coffee for the machine, but that would happen after breakfast. If he found that, they could stop drinking the instant coffee. Considering everything that had happened over the last twenty-four hours, Nik was surprised both he and Morgan were awake. He attributed being awake mostly to sitting in the office upstairs with Morgan, discussing the case and Oscar and all the shit in between.

"So what do federal witnesses and their bodyguards do for fun here?" Morgan asked. He raked a hand through his wet hair, and Nik watched as it spiked up and stayed spiky. Morgan hadn't shaved. A five o'clock shadow darkened his face, but he looked bright eyed and ready for whatever the day threw at them.

"We have a satellite for television, maybe movies?"

Morgan flexed the muscles in his arms. "I need some exercise, man. This sitting around shit is turning muscle to fat."

Nik swallowed his instinctive response to say that actually Morgan looked gorgeous. He continued quickly.

"There's the lake. You could sit there or go swimming or something." Morgan brightened considerably.

"I would love that. Hell, I was on the swim team in high school. I can go in the water, right?" He glanced sideways at his arm and wrinkled his nose in question.

"It's fine if the water is clean and we cover the wound with plastic like when you showered."

"Thank fuck for that. I wasn't even allowed out in Albany. I imagine you will need to keep an eye out for lake monsters or mutant pike, in case they eat me." The last he said with a smirk on his face, and it was a wonder to see it first thing in the morning. Morgan had the enthusiasm of a young kid, and suddenly Nik felt older than his almost thirty years.

"All part of my job description."

"Monster watching?"

"Completely," he deadpanned, laughter being held back with force.

"My hero." It was nice… No, wrong word to use. It was refreshing to flirt like this, different, new, and most definitely what they were doing. Most of Nik's relationships had started in the dark at clubs, and to be honest, most of them had ended in the same places. He hadn't done a lot of out-and-out flirting before.

"Gotta be good for something," he pointed out.

"And we are really allowed out?" Morgan reminded Nik of a kitten his family had adopted when he was around ten. The calico had sat at the patio windows miaowing to be allowed out almost from day one. Its instincts were to be outside in the air, and Nik got the same vibe from Morgan.

"Not like anyone is going to come up here and find us," he pointed out succinctly. Morgan finished his toast in two mouthfuls, swallowed his remaining coffee and grew visibly impatient as Nik took a longer time to clear his plate and mug.

Within five minutes the two men were standing in the tangled, weed-choked, and overgrown yard, which to Nik's eye may well have been a garden at some point in its history. At the very least, it had a couple of borders. Maybe it had been used by the first owners of the ramshackled cabin's outer casing. Possibly to grow vegetables, fruit, or even flowers. He couldn't imagine anyone wanting to grow regimented lines of flowers in such an interweave of wilderness and water, but to each their own.

The path to the other wooden structure they had seen from the window was so overgrown it was difficult to make out if it was a path at all. Somehow they made it to the shore, which Nik judged was no more than forty feet from the house. The white-barked paper birch trees and low-lying baby sugar maples draped in beautiful disarray over the still lake, and the shade was chilly on the skin in the new morning. The water itself was clean, or at least it appeared to be, and he thought back to what Morgan had said when they first arrived.

"You said something about glaciers, I remember." Morgan stopped what he was doing, hunched in a crouch, running his fingers through the water at the edge of the lake. He looked embarrassed for a second then seemed to struggle with a decision. He colored with a flush of embarrassment before starting to talk.

"Geology. It's a hobby of mine, I guess. I read a lot of *National Geographic*. This lake is what I think they call a kettle hole, or kettle pond."

"And how do the glaciers fit in with that?" Nik prompted gently.

"The last glacier through here caused all of this." Morgan waved his hand, indicating the lake spreading away from them. "It was kind of young really. They called it the Wisconsin; it passed here only ten thousand years ago. When it thawed, huge chunks of the ice broke off, and they were buried beneath accumulating sand and gravel." He stopped talking to scramble to his feet, looking out over the water. "When those chunks of ice melted, they left depressions in the landscape with the gravel and sand sinking." He paused again, and looked away from Nik.

"Go on," Nik encouraged.

"When a hole went below the water table, then the pond is made and it's constantly topped up with fresh water higher in the mountains."

"Okay," was all Nik could say, not so much at the words but at the animation in Morgan's entire body.

"Yeah, I know, I'm a dork."

"No, it's interesting. I didn't know anything about glaciers up here in the mountains, and now I do."

"So next time you are staring down the end of a gun you can dazzle the bad guys with your knowledge of kettle holes." Morgan was clearly trying to be witty, but the words were a stark reminder of his job, and it jolted him back to the here and now.

"Will my bandage be okay if I go swimming?"

Morgan looked uncertainly at his arm, the edge of white showing under his short sleeves.

Nik nodded. "We'll cover it with the plastic again. Should be fine as long as you really think this water is clean." He peered at the water doubtfully. He could see the bottom here at the edge and it looked clear, but who knew what was in the middle of Lake Dante? It wouldn't look good if Morgan died, not at the hands of the bad guys, but because Nik had allowed him to swim in a polluted lake. Shaking his head to clear that train of thought, Nik went back to the cabin and came out clutching plastic and tape. Morgan pulled his T-shirt carefully over his head, wincing only momentarily when the material snagged on the bandage, but finally was standing there naked from the waist up. It was another view Nik couldn't take his eyes away from, and when Morgan removed the rest of his clothes and stood there in only cotton boxers, it was all Nik could do not to scoop him up and take him indoors. Jeez, was he that sex starved he was lusting after a kid he was supposed to be protecting? He focused on taping the plastic, and then with a word of warning to Morgan as to not bumping his arm or overdoing it, he stood back.

Thinking about his charge in a sexual way was inappropriate, unsafe, and very wrong.

"Last one in…" Morgan waded in until he was about six feet from shore, turning back briefly and flashing a wide grin before duck-diving below the water and then appearing at the surface a way out. He began swimming towards the far end of the small lake, no more than a football field in length but still farther than Nik realized he was entirely comfortable with.

He would get in if he could. He liked swimming as much as the next man, but three things stopped him. The first was the Glock nestled in the small of his back and covered by his shirt. He wasn't entirely comfortable here yet, and the gun was his reassurance he could handle anything thrown at them. He knew from experience it would be a good two days before he could fully trust the safety of Sanctuary Seven. The second reason was the water was probably freaking cold, but that, he guessed, could be a good thing in helping him with his third thing —the fact that he had been half hard since Morgan had found him in the office. Seeing Morgan, with his lithe-muscled swimmer's body, as good as naked in clinging boxers that left nothing to the imagination, had sent all his blood south before his brain had anything to say on the matter.

You don't have relationships with clients, and you don't compromise their safety because your eye was off the ball. It had been drummed into him from day one with the feds, and it was a rule that had served him well so far. Problem was, until now, it had been easy. With a combination of small families, older men or the occasion when he'd guarded a woman, he had only been left in charge of one single man before—the prostitute with the drug problem who made him crazy. Certainly no attraction there.

Morgan reached the other side of the lake and turned to swim back, stopping half way, at the point Nik imagined it was deepest, and then like an otter, he was diving and surfacing. It was unbridled enthusiasm and peace, and Nik realized something fundamental as he watched with his hand behind him resting on the Glock. He wanted that enthusiasm under him in bed far too much to give in to the thoughts and allow himself the luxury of sinking into his charge.

Sighing, he positioned himself on the edge of a wooden plank, moving until he had the balance of it just right, and watched. He was good at watching.

Chapter Eight

THE LAKE WAS DEEP IN THE CENTER OF THE KETTLE hole, probably as much as forty feet, maybe more, and the water was so clear Morgan could see to dive and view the lakebed. He couldn't make it all the way to the bottom with his arm injured, and it had started to ache so he satisfied himself with diving and swimming just below the surface. The water was icy and clear, and there was the usual collection of stuff you would find at the bottom of a lake—gravel, large stones, the odd boulder —but there was no rubbish like there had been in the lakes he used to swim in as a kid. No bicycles, or tires, or bricks. It was beautiful. He swam to the side and ducked under the surface, pushing aside branches fallen from the trees above. Part of the joy of swimming in the open, in lakes and rivers, was to unearth what had lain undisturbed under the water for so long.

Every time he surfaced, he glanced over to where Nik was standing. The bodyguard was a solid presence among the ruins of the jetty, and he was staring out over the water. Serious and clearly in full-on protector mode, he made an incredibly sexy picture, and if Morgan didn't know better, it looked posed.

He wasn't swimming enough to keep heat in his body, his arm telegraphing that it really wasn't handling the exercise or the cold at all well, and he began a lazy crawl back to where Nik sat. He hesitated as the water level dropped to waist height, adjusting his boxers to stop them dragging down with the weight of water, and then casually began to climb out over the twigs and stones collected on the small shore.

"Cold?" Nik's voice sounded strained, and with a shiver, Morgan shrugged.

"Not too bad. I'm getting a warm shower. You coming?" He could have bitten his tongue off. The cold had obviously affected his brain. "I didn't mean you… and me… in the… Shit." Angry at his near teenage levels of embarrassment and his runaway mouth, he collected his clothes and began to walk back to the cabin. He didn't know what was worse—that Nik hadn't said anything, or that he wished Nik *had* said something. All he heard was a low chuckle and then the sounds of boots crunching through undergrowth. It was slow going for Morgan. With prickles pushing into the soles of his feet and exasperated, he dropped his sneakers and slipped bare feet into them.

"Nice look," Nik offered, and narrow-eyed, Morgan turned to him.

"I make sneakers and boxers look hot," he said, realizing Nik wasn't looking at his sneakers but directly at his cotton-wrapped ass.

If he added a wiggle to his walk when he strode ahead then he couldn't be held responsible. He was a gay man and had received a frank look of appreciation so it was natural to react.

———

SHOWER FINISHED, he dressed in sweats and a t-shirt he found in the closet. He asked Nik to re-bandage the arm, and tiredness stole across him as the meds kicked in and the swimming took its toll. Nik was doing something in the kitchen, making coffee, clattering around. The sofa in the main room, with a good view of the kitchen in one direction and the trees in the other, was a huge comfy cloud of goodness. The dreams that had woken him this morning seemed to be there waiting for him again as soon as he gave in to sleep. This time he couldn't hide from the images of blood and death in the alleyway when he ran from being shot, or from the stark images of the shooter's uniform and the realization it was a cop who was killing the victim. He hated these dreams, interwoven with sense memories of the hard stone wall against his back, the keys that fell to the ground.

He needed those keys; every single one of them was important, and in his dream, instead of running, he stooped to collect them together, making sure each one lined up with the next, shuffling them into order of size. The order of them was important, even as the guy held a gun to his head. He looked up at the man smiling down at him and heard the noise of the safety being released. Why wasn't he able to run? Why did his dreams stop him from running?

He hated this dream. The decisions he'd made on that day, the ones that had allowed him to live, were turned about-face every single time he shut his eyes. The guy with the flint hard eyes, the cop he knew now as Headley, was shaking his arm, talking to him. Calling his name.

"Morgan..." He didn't want to open his eyes, but the voice was insistent. "You're dreaming... Wake up, Morgan." Suddenly very much awake, he jerked out of sleep with a curse to see Nik's face inches away from his, and his good arm in a firm grip.

"Don't wake up people in the middle of dreaming," he grumped irritably, his mouth dry and his arm throbbing in pain. Nik shook his head.

"It's sleepwalkers you don't disturb."

"I needed sleep. Don't wake me the fuck up."

"You were talking and shaking. That isn't proper sleep. Do you think you want to maybe talk about the dreams?" God, *psychoanalyst* Nik's voice was so damned understanding that it grated on Morgan. Trapped in the last vestiges of sleep, he let the irritation snap out with another curse.

"I don't need to talk about my dreams. Why don't you fuck off and leave me alone?"

Nik did just that, clambering to stand and then crossing to the kitchen where he had been when Morgan had fallen asleep. Shame at his flash of temper bit Morgan hard, and he sank back into the soft cushions, closing his eyes and ashamed of his reaction. The last thing he wanted to do was share any of the shit in his head with Mr Hard-Assed Bodyguard, so he should stop with the asking. It wasn't like him to lose his temper. In fact, anyone would say Morgan Drake didn't even have a temper. What was it about Nik that had lit a fuse under him just then?

He registered the scent of something from the kitchen, and his stomach rumbled. Glancing at his wrist for the time, he remembered he didn't have a watch or a cell, or anything to judge his day by. It looked darker outside, indicating it was into evening, which meant he had slept for at least eight hours or so.

"Hungry?" Nik didn't seem pissed with him, which oddly enough wound Morgan up even further.

"Don't do that," he snapped.

"Do what?" Nik sounded so damn innocent. Morgan joined him in the kitchen, stretching out muscles and scratching his itching stubble.

"The whole, 'it's okay, Morgan, I understand, and do you want to talk about it?' crap. You don't understand, and I don't need to talk about it."

"Okay—"

"A woman was shot in the head in front of me by a gun-wielding maniac, who actually wasn't a maniac but was cold as ice and who then turned the gun on me. I am sure as hell going to have dreams about that kind of shit."

"I know it's—"

"So I don't need you to sit and analyze me or my dreams." Morgan took a step closer to Nik, getting right into his space, the smell of tomato sauce wafting up from a silver saucepan.

"All I want to do is get my head around the case. I'm not actually—"

"Stop asking me to talk about it all." There he'd said it. Nik nodded and then reached for the stove controls, turning off the heat under the saucepan.

"I promise you," he started gently, turning to face Morgan with his hands out in front of him, palms upward, "I won't ask you to talk about any of it." Nik's voice was calm, gentle even.

"Shit, Nik, quit with the pansy-ass understanding crap. I thought you were supposed to be some kind of tough guy." Morgan was aware he was making little sense, but he was still only half awake.

"Morgan—"

"I don't need a psychiatrist watching my back. I need someone who will make sure I am alive to testify." They were in a weird kind of standoff, Nik's features calm and Morgan bristling with irritation.

"I'll keep you alive." Such a simple statement, delivered with utter conviction and certainty.

"Good," Morgan snapped back in an instant. "I'm not a girl, and I can process the shit in my head fine without interference."

"I happen to have some experience in this kind of thing, if you felt like you needed a friend," Nik added.

"I don't give a shit; I'm not talking. I'm handling it fine."

"You don't need to talk. I can imagine exactly what the dreams are like. I've seen things that stay with me when I shut my eyes."

Morgan so desperately wanted to throw a "whatever"

at the guy who was supposedly the last line of defense between him and a bullet. But the way Nik had worded it begged for elaboration, and his curiosity got the better of him.

"You have?" he finally asked.

"I've seen people die before. It's the nature of the job." The words were spoken as a simple matter of fact. Nik shrugged, like it was no big thing, except the set of his face and a flicker of something in his eyes told a different story. Morgan didn't need to discuss seeing a defenseless woman take a bullet in the head, right through the eye, half her face carved away, blood on the ground, on the walls, in fact blood everywhere. That wasn't an image he needed to share with anyone. It wouldn't hurt to get Nik's handle on the dreams though.

"Know what's really fucked?" he started. "When I finally relax enough to fall asleep, I'm back there in the alley watching her die, and I don't run. I stand frozen, and I *wait* for the guy to shoot me too."

"Like your feet are encased in concrete." Nik was nodding.

"Yeah, exactly. I drop all my keys, and they all separate from the key ring. In my dream, I pick the stuff up. Can you believe it? I actually take the time, with a gun inches from me, to pick up the damn keys. Keys that mean nothing, that are nothing." His headache was worse, but at least the racing in his heart had lessened.

"There isn't a mention on your files of you being shot at. I'm guessing, in reality, you left the keys. Right?"

"Fuck yes, I left them. The woman was dead; her

face was gone, and I ran through five alleys, places I knew, and then I hid."

"You ran, and for that reason alone, you stayed alive and can now give evidence against the man who killed an innocent victim."

Morgan was rooted to the spot as completely as he'd been in his dreams, staring into deep brown eyes filled with compassion, and a single layer of the shell around his fears fractured and loosened.

"I don't want to talk any more about the dreams," Morgan repeated.

"Okay, well, let's eat then. Could you eat now?"

"What is it?" Morgan indicated the pasta next to the saucepan and then lifted the lid to the other pan to reveal boiling water.

"Just pasta and sauce."

Food, Morgan would tell anyone who cared to listen, was the one thing that could make even the worst things better. Yes, he had a headache, and, yes, his mind was still confused and woolly, but pasta and sauce sounded like manna from heaven.

Dinner was good, the beer was cold, and the conversation was easy. Morgan finally felt himself relaxing in Nik's company even though he still didn't have a good handle on the man Nik was. What experiences had he had in his life that made him the best man to look after Morgan. Where Taylor had been an open book, overtly guarding him with room sweeps, studying case notes, making calls, asking questions, Nik appeared steadier and quieter. It still didn't make the man any less dangerous. Taylor had been shot, fallen to the floor, and still managed to twist his body to protect Morgan and kill the bad guy at the same time, with a bullet right between the assailant's eyes. Nik hadn't shown any expertise in the whole guarding business as yet, but Taylor wouldn't have sent him here if he didn't think Nik could handle it.

By silent agreement they stayed away from discussing the case, the shooting, or how Morgan felt. They discussed football, basketball, being a fed, being an office worker, anything and everything. They worked in companionable silence as they cleaned the kitchen, which didn't take long, and then Nik pulled a soda and a beer out of the huge fridge.

Morgan nursed his new beer. The first one had given him a good buzz, but that was probably because he hadn't had a proper drink in weeks. He leaned back against the counter, watching Nik stack dishes.

"I didn't grow up wanting to work in an office, you know." Where that had come from Morgan didn't know, and he cursed the beer for loosening his tongue.

"I didn't mean any offense when I said that," Nik replied immediately. A warmth stole into Morgan at the frown on Nik's face.

"I know you didn't. I don't imagine there were very many kids who desperately want to work in administration." Nik nodded and then moved to lean back against the counter.

"So what did Morgan Drake want to do?"

"Draw. Paint. Animation, cartoons, even serious stuff."

"So why didn't you?"

"My step-dad was in and out of hospital my last year at school. I put college on hold, stayed around, got the job in the cubicle; he died, and I never left. Got used to having money and I had my own small apartment."

"Life can be like that. Throws you curve balls."

"I bet you always wanted to be a cop."

"An astronaut actually. But the feds were recruiting out of college, and it was good money. 'Course I was also shit at physics."

"But you enjoy what you do now?" Morgan was insistent; he wanted to know that.

"Yeah, for the most part. Plays hell with the sex life." That last bit was clearly something Nik hadn't meant to say, and he ducked his head. The big, tall, hulking bodyguard was embarrassed.

Morgan wanted nothing more than to step forward and offer himself up on a plate. He didn't. Instead, he suggested a film from the extensive DVD collection under the TV. Nik seemed relieved at the change in subject and agreed readily to watch *The Shawshank Redemption.*

Film over, both men thoughtful, it was time for more sleep. Morgan felt like he was all slept out. But the minute his head hit the pillow and the lockdown echoed through the cabin, he felt sleep pulling him under.

Chapter Nine

"IT'S NOT IDEAL, BUT I MANAGED TO FIND THIS." NIK handed over the spoils of his investigation to Morgan, who sat disconsolately on the tumbled wood of the jetty. It was day five, and the swimming wasn't filling the entire day, so apart from his skin pinking in whatever sun there was, it wasn't enough to keep Morgan's attention. Morgan looked up at what Nik had brought out and accepted the pad of plain paper gratefully. He had mentioned the art thing, and suddenly Nik was adamant he could find paper and art supplies for Morgan. After all, there had been kids hidden here at some point.

"Did you find any pencils?"

"Just normal pencils, but... umm..." He wasn't sure how Morgan would react to this one. It was probably a stupid idea. "I found some coloring pencils in the kids' box." He pulled the pack of twelve pencils out of his pocket and held them steadily for Morgan to take.

"Oh my god," Morgan said. Grabbing at the pencils, he opened the pack and examined the contents, running a finger from red to yellow to green to purple. "This is so cool. Thank you."

"They're okay?"

"They work; I can use them."

Nik crouched down in front of him. "The files say you have shown some of your art."

Morgan nodded at this and then shrugged. "I love sketching, but I'm no artist. I had a few exhibitions when I was younger, but art doesn't pay the bills."

"Hence staying at the cubicle job for the rest of your life?"

"Yeah, it pays the bills."

"What are you going to sketch?"

"The lake, the trees, you." He added the last with a hopeful smile, and something turned in Nik's chest. Morgan really had the most intriguing eyes, and they were gazing up at him, looking so damn confident he would pull it off.

"In your dreams, pencil geek," Nik said firmly and strode back to the house, the sound of Morgan's chuckling following him back to the door. There was no freaking way he would sit still all day as some model. He connected to Ops via the encrypted satellite phone; there was nothing new on the case, and the threat level was low. No one appeared to have one iota of an idea where Morgan was being hidden. He requested some extra information on the Bullens and on the cop Headley, then made coffees. He checked the Glock at the back of his jeans and then grabbed a book and the two mugs, wandering back to the lake. Morgan was hunched over the pad, his hands swapping pencils as a sketch formed.

Nik didn't want to interrupt, but he did peer over Morgan's shoulder to see what he was drawing. It was a representation of trees, very nicely done if a bit basic to start with and he placed the coffee down with a murmured, "Coffee."

He settled in the V formed by the roots of two trees, dead opposite Morgan, his back to one of the trunks and the novel in his lap. Despite the level of vigilance that formed his constant companion, he felt a small amount of relaxation washing over him. They sat that way for a few hours, and he managed to make it through at least three chapters of the book. He couldn't remember the last time he had read any more than the dust jacket on any novel he was interested in. He realized he had moved into the world he was reading about when a shadow fell over him and he was startled by Morgan dropping to a crouch in front of him.

"Hey, protector, you snoozing? Wanna see?" He held out the pad, and Nik grasped it, turning it around to see the sketch of the lake. It was gorgeous and accurate, details picked out in colors in the trees and the sun sparkling off of the water. Morgan reached and turned to the next page, and Nik just stared. It was all he could do when faced with a pencil sketch of himself sprawled against the tree, his face intent on the book on his knees. What could he say? Somehow in a few pencil strokes, Morgan had captured a likeness of Nik he actually recognized and made him look, at the same time, really different.

"You're good."

"It's easy when I have a good model." Morgan's eyes,

so blue, so damn earnest, were inches from his as he examined the sketch from the side. He traced the drawn face with a finger. "Who'd've thought Mr Hard Man would be so pretty, eh? You have very interesting features, all sharp and angled, and then this incredible bone structure."

"Yeah, right." He remembered the last of his one or two lovers, more fuck buddies if he was honest. They liked him because he was strong, and certain, and in control. Not one of them waxed lyrical about his bone structure. Morgan looked at him sharply with confusion in his eyes.

"You don't see that?"

Nik squirmed, suddenly uncomfortable with the scrutiny, and with a noise of frustration, he scrambled to stand. "I'm going in. You need to come in as well. I'll start lunch." He knew he was being unfair. He even caught a brief look of hurt flashing across Morgan's face, but hell, he was a man doing a man's job. He didn't need the drawing and the comments and the fancy words.

He strode into the cabin and looked pointedly at Morgan until the other man made his way to the structure. Nik didn't relax until the door was shut behind them. Annoyed with his lack of composure, he excused himself and moved up to the office. Maybe an hour of trawling through case files before lunch would settle his thoughts and calm down his libido. Startling blue eyes had a way of seeing into his soul, and damn the man for throwing flowery crap at him.

"I'm sorry, Nik," Morgan said gently from the door. "I didn't mean to make you uncomfortable." Nik sighed inwardly. Morgan had this kicked puppy voice, and Nik knew if he turned, his charge would have an expression to match. "Everyone always says I am too honest and that I say things I shouldn't."

Nik pushed his chair away from his desk and swiveled to face Morgan.

"You didn't make me feel uncomfortable. I just don't like to be laughed at."

Morgan frowned, stepping in to the room and coming to stand right in front of him. "I wasn't laughing at you."

"All that *pretty* shit wasn't laughing? Yeah, right. Look, it doesn't matter. It's a good sketch, maybe you can send it to my mom."

He made to move back to the computer and *oofed* as he suddenly got a lapful of Morgan and the chair slid back to hit the table. For a second he thought the chair would snap in two under their combined weight, and he could no more hold back his instant reaction than he could save them if the two of them fell to the floor.

"What the hell?"

Morgan wriggled astride him as if he was getting comfortable, and it was all Nik could do not to upend him on his ass to the floor. Stunned at what had happened, and still not entirely sure what was going on, he placed his hands on Morgan's hips to assist him in standing. Morgan wriggled again to get balanced. *Jeez,* he thought, *enough with the wriggling.* Then all he was capable of doing was holding his breath as Morgan used his free hands to trace Nik's face.

"See? You have really good bones." He touched

Nik's cheekbones, moving up to caress his eyelashes, causing Nik to close his eyes as he flinched.

"Morgan," he growled, "you have to get the hell off me." He moved his hands lower to get a good grip of butt cheek and thigh, coiling to lift and push in one move. Then he stopped at Morgan's next words.

"You have this mouth, Mr Hero Guy. I just want to taste it. It's so pretty, strong but soft, and your eyes are deep velvet brown, and your lashes are so long. And then your chin, so square and so damned stubborn. You are this whole confusion of hard and soft." Nik searched for a response; he was coming up blank. "Can I?" Morgan added.

"Can you what?"

"Can I taste you?"

"Morgan—" *This is the worst idea in the history of bad ideas. Morgan is a client, Morgan is a freaking client.*

"Please." Morgan leaned forward, and Nik went from half erect to iron in seconds, with Morgan's dick hard against him and the soft caress of his breath on Nik's lips.

"One," Nik heard himself say. One kiss would surely be enough to get Morgan off his lap, but he didn't believe he had consciously made the decision to agree to anything. Morgan was clearly compelling him. Somehow.

"One," Morgan whispered, placing a gentle kiss on one corner of Nik's mouth and then sliding his lips to the other corner. He leaned back, leaving his hands to cup Nik's face. "Can I do it again?" He sounded worried, and it was the worry that cut through Nik's daze. In one unceremonious shove, he pushed Morgan off his lap, watching as *his client* stumbled to regain his balance, a look of dismay and surprise on his face.

"No," Nik snapped, making to turn back to the screen of his computer.

"Please."

He stopped the chair's motion at Morgan's simple *please*. "You don't throw yourself at total strangers, Morgan. You fuck with my head, and you end up dead. I can't protect you and fuck you at the same time," he said crudely.

"Nik, wait." Nik did, in fact, wait. All he wanted was to give himself time to breathe. He waited and watched as Morgan held up a single finger and mouthed "one second". Turning on his heel, Morgan crossed to the panel on the wall and pressed his code. Lockdown occurred immediately, and in a matter of moments, he had climbed back on to Nik's lap, twisting his hands around the back of Nik's neck.

"What the fuck?"

"We're safe in here so you can stand down, hero," Morgan said simply. "Now we can fuck." He leaned down and continued the kiss, this time harder, more insistent, and Nik didn't know what to do, stop or continue, pull him closer or push him away. He opened his mouth to protest at the lapful of squirming client forcing him to interact, but Morgan took advantage, his tongue sliding into the space and beginning to taste. A full body shudder ran through Morgan, and Nik could no more push the man off him than he could stop. He tilted his face, deepening the kiss and placing his hands where he wanted to, squarely on Morgan's butt, pulling him closer. Morgan eased back to look down at him, and it gave Nik a moment to think.

"We shouldn't be—"

"Are you going to give me the Costner speech from *The Bodyguard*? Like you can't protect me—"

"My mind needs to be on the job."

"One job at a time, hero."

"Look, if we're going to do anything, I need a shower."

"I like my men wet," Morgan teased, capturing Nik's lips in another heated kiss.

"'M serious," Nik forced out, and Morgan sighed before grinding one last time and then clambering off.

"I'll be in my room." Morgan smirked, leaving the office with a definite swagger, and Nik blinked at the retreating man. What the hell had he just said? What the hell was he doing? He was getting a cold shower to batten down his libido, and then he was out of here for air. Compromising Morgan's safety in this way was way beyond stupid and entering into a physical relationship with someone he was supposed to be protecting was plain suicide. He adjusted himself—still so damn hard—and concentrated on his Great Aunt Cherry from his childhood with the hairy chin and gray whiskers. It did wonders, and within five minutes, he was standing in the bathroom with only half a hard-on, running the water until it was warm to wash and climbing in as it heated to the temperature he liked. He would get clean and then turn it around to cold. That would take care of the problem of the dick that threatened to ruin everything.

He might have known his idiot client wouldn't stay put. The shower door swung open, and there stood Morgan, his bandage covered in plastic, naked as the day he was born and fully erect. Beautiful, lithe, toned. He stepped into the shower with a grin and then embraced Nik.

"You said you were going to be in your room," Nik managed to say between kisses, suddenly wondering why he was even starting this conversation when he had an armful of hot, naked Morgan.

"I was bored 'cause you took so long." He kissed Nik, the warm water running over them both. "I like showers." His mouth moved to Nik's ear, gently biting and teasing a path from neck to earlobe. He whispered in a low growl, "Trust me."

Nik wasn't sure what Morgan meant but nearly swallowed his tongue when Morgan unhooked the shower hose and head and adjusted it to a gentle spray. Carefully and systematically, he washed his lover's body, paying particular attention to Nik's dick.

"Fuck" was all Nik could coherently string together in the way of a sentence, one word for a sensual experience. Morgan wasn't finished yet though. Oh hell no. It seemed he had planned a whole new level of torture for Nik.

Morgan went to his knees. "Trust me," he whispered again, and then his voice took a more direct, steely tone. "Move your legs apart," he ordered firmly, and then Nik could think of nothing as Morgan licked a strip from balls to tip and then closed his mouth around the head of Nik's cock, gently teasing with his lips and tongue. Nik loved receiving head as much as the next guy, but the view as he looked down, Morgan's hair slick to his head, tendrils falling on his forehead, his blue eyes wide and fueled by lust, was stunning.

Nik whimpered as Morgan maneuvered the shower head and directed the gentle spray on Nik's balls, nearly making him come there and then. The gentle teasing of his cock with the spray on his sac was like no blowjob he had ever had from a lover before. The water's caress was such a deep, sensual feeling, and the full-on attention his cock was now receiving from Morgan led him to an orgasm more deep and intense than he had ever experienced. Why had he never thought of using a shower like this? It was like having all the benefits of an extra person in the shower, paying you all the attention, but without the space or jealousy issues.

Added to which Morgan had swallowed everything Nik had to give, and fuck if that wasn't the icing on the whole thing. Boneless, he stumbled back against the tiles, and Morgan scrambled to stand, looping his arms around Nik's neck, the discarded shower hose spraying their feet. It was clear Morgan wanted more kisses, and Nik wasn't going to hold back.

"Fuckin' hot." Nik was proud of his ability to create a sentence.

"It's a trick I learned from watching too much porn."

"We need to do that again."

"We will. But right now… I'm…" He indicated with a nod downwards to where his dick strained rigid against his stomach and one of his hands was circling and moving. Nik turned off the water, grabbed a towel, and passed it cursorily over long tangled hair, then just grabbed Morgan's hand and pulled him out of the bathroom and to the closest bedroom; his.

"Condoms—" he began quickly.

"I already swallowed—" Morgan touched a finger to his lips.

Nik could feel heat rising in his face at the memory. "No sense in chancing it again."

"I'm clean."

"I am too, but, Morgan, we don't know. Either one of us could be lying. Let's just—"

"Okay. Okay. I'm not arguing." Morgan scrambled backwards and up the bed, and Nik nearly swallowed his tongue. Morgan was one fine-looking man, all carved and lithe with strong muscled legs. He shook his head, opening the smaller medical box, pulling out condoms, and dropping one on the bed. He wasn't used to this. Lovers looked to him to lead, to top, but they hadn't ascertained what was happening here. He had switched before, but—

"Stop over-thinking and come make love to me."

It was an invitation Nik couldn't refuse, and he climbed Morgan's body until he leaned over him, Morgan's hands caught in his, kissing until breathing was hard. Nik pulled back. There were acres of skin he just had to taste, so he bent to kiss-bite along muscled ridges. He stopped at each nipple, sucking and marking smooth skin, then moving back up to chase a kiss. Morgan whimpered into his mouth, hard against him.

"Nik..." Morgan moaned into kisses, pulling at trapped hands, twisting under him, his neck arched and his throat exposed for kisses. Nik twisted a hand into Morgan's short hair and spent a long time kissing and pressing his own hard dick against Morgan, savoring the gasps from the other man. He knew exactly where to take this next and released his hold in Morgan's hair so he could concentrate on tracking his own path of kisses down to Morgan's leaking dick. He reached for lube and slicked his fingers. One, then the second and the third, stretching gently, opening up his lover. He concentrated his tongue and lips on Morgan, loving the taste of him, the texture of him, and crooking his finger to find the gland he knew would send Morgan flying.

The single touch was enough to send Morgan arching up off the bed, crying out, and he started to lose it, an incoherent mess of want and need.

"Stop—I'll come—please—"

Nik continued tasting and licking, climbing back up Morgan's body and demanding a sloppy, messy kiss. His movements were fast, jerky, a jumble of confused kisses and words whispered against each other's breaths, *fuck, want you*. Taking a few seconds to put on a condom he waited and looked down at Morgan who had closed his eyes. Nik eased inside, gently rocking a small amount each time until he lay inside, balls deep. Morgan's blue eyes opened, and his face was flushed. Discomfort, then raw need was etched onto every line.

"Move," Morgan ordered, breathless, plainly desperate for some kind of friction, his dick pressed between them, his own hand reaching. Nik's rhythm was broken; his eyes shut tight. There were no kisses, merely exchanges of breath in open mouths gasping for air. Nik could feel Morgan's hand on his own dick, twisting and pulling, and then he felt the heat between them as Morgan lost it hot and wet between them.

It was hard and fast and over so quickly. Morgan's orgasm sent Nik over the edge and he keened as he pulled his head back, his own climax explosive. He never came so close together with a lover. It was more sensation than content, but jeez if it wasn't the hottest thing he had ever done.

"Fuck—" Nik kissed sweat damp skin, swallowing any reply Morgan might make to the exclamation, pulling out and falling utterly completed to one side.

The heat subsided, the semen became cool and wet between them, and Nik knew they needed to clean up but he wasn't able to move. Morgan took the initiative, grabbing at a shirt from the floor and wiping them as best he could, then he nestled back into Nik's hold. It was in that position Morgan fell asleep, with Nik not long behind him.

———

NIK WOKE first and lay there for a long time simply staring at the man who had turned his life upside down, until Morgan's eyes opened.

"You look tired still," Nik said softly, his hand reaching out of its own accord to brush Morgan's hair away from his forehead. Neither said a word as Nik's hand slid down the side of Morgan's face and rested on his neck, pressing gently, smoothing away the stress. "You didn't sleep so well," he added.

Morgan frowned. "I didn't?"

"You couldn't lie still, kept moving" *Kept pulling me to you, pulling me close.*

"'M sorry if I kept you awake," Morgan apologized quickly.

There was silence again as Nik leaned down until his lips hovered a breath from Morgan, then he dropped the lightest of kisses into the soft dark hair. "You didn't, Morgan, you didn't." He moved slightly to pull Morgan back against him, securing his hands round his chest and letting him relax back, Morgan's bed hair tickling at his nose. "It was fine."

Morgan yawned widely and then settled back to sleep. Nik couldn't have stayed awake if he'd tried.

———

"DO we need to talk about this?" Morgan's voice was clear and firm, and pulled Nik from the last vestiges of sleep. He blinked and looked up at his client, his lover, who was sitting cross-legged next to him. It took a while to focus, and he waited until he could see every expression that crossed Morgan's face. He was confused. Hadn't they already talked this morning? He had a sketchy memory of telling Morgan he hadn't slept well— thought it was okay. Or if not entirely okay then somewhat of an acceptable situation.

"Do we?" He threw the question back at Morgan,

coughing at the gruffness in his own voice. Morgan tilted his head and stared at Nik appraisingly.

"Look. The way I see it…"

Nik moved to lie on one side, his head propped up with his hand. *This should be interesting.*

"It's another eight days to go of enforced isolation, right?"

"Eight, less about five hours." *To be exact.*

"Then I give evidence, and depending what goes down, my life goes back to normal or I get shot. Are you with me so far?"

"With you."

"Well, you may never see me again, 'cause I'll be off hiding myself away as Abraham Wallis from Connecticut with a degree in Nerd, and I'll probably even turn heterosexual." Morgan shivered delicately, and Nik smiled to himself. Morgan made him laugh. "Either that, or… Hell, your bodyguarding thing doesn't make for an efficient social life, I'm guessing."

"True, I—"

"So," Morgan interrupted, "we have two healthy gay males in a cabin in the ass-end of absolutely nowhere, with a beautiful lake, enough food for an army, and our choice of three comfortable beds. We have at least four boxes of condoms I know about and three bottles of lube, not to mention the olive oil in the kitchen."

Olive oil? Interesting. "Okay."

"We should just… you know… enjoy the days we have." The poor guy was seriously verging on blushing, and the teasing side of Nik rose to the surface.

"In a hot, dirty sexual kind of way," Nik attempted to clarify, with a smirk

"Absolutely, totally."

"And in return, and this is deadly serious, if I think you are in danger and I say jump, all I want to hear is you saying 'how high?'."

"Agreed, but can I ask you one thing before we embark on eight days of shagging like bunnies?" Morgan talked like he was making a joke, but his serious expression belied the fact.

"Go on." Nik was cautious, wondering exactly what it was Morgan wanted to discuss that could in any way match the serious expression on his client's face.

"I want to be serious, 'cause, as much as I want to climb your body and let you do wicked things to me," he paused, lowering his gaze, his voice suddenly quieter, "will doing this really compromise your safety? Compromise mine?"

Nik swallowed his immediate answer. Morgan was demanding honesty, and Nik owed him the real answer.

"When we are in lockdown, very little can get in here, apart from someone with a code, or indeed some kind of armor-piercing weapon." Morgan blanched, and Nik wished he could bite off his tongue, realizing his explanation probably didn't need to be quite so graphic. He sighed. "Anything that takes my eye off the ball is a compromise on keeping you safe, Morgan." Nik wasn't ready to go into specifics. Staying detached from your client was important; it allowed you to think clearly. He already had affection for Morgan, but it wasn't so much that it would cloud his judgment at the current levels. It was Nik's job to protect Morgan. He was the last line of defense between Morgan and a bullet, a car, a knife, or any of a million ways Morgan could be killed. Nothing that happened between them physically would stop Nik being that defense. Nothing.

The unpredictable part was what *Morgan* would do if they found themselves in a situation where Nik was in danger. It was *Nik's* job to be in danger. Inevitably, to keep Morgan *out* of harm's way, it might well mean putting himself in danger.

"I mean it, Morgan. If something was to happen between where we are now and the hearing, I want you to tell me you will keep your head down, and do what I tell you."

"I promise." The expression on his face reminded Nik of his nephew's face before Christmas, promising to be good. Uncurling his body and legs, he leaned over Nik and placed the gentlest of kisses on his lips.

Against his better judgment Nik deepened the kiss. His acceptance of where this was going—of what was happening—could never be spoken more eloquently than by the action of him reaching up and twisting his free hand into Morgan's hair.

The noise of his cell interrupted the kiss, breaking through the jumbled thoughts and emotions swirling in his head, and reluctantly, he pulled away to reach for it.

"Valentinov," he said, wriggling away from Morgan's hand, which had slyly wrapped around his dick. He needed to concentrate on what Ops wanted, and he threw a quick censorious glance at Morgan, who returned the look with a benign smile.

"Can you talk?" Something about the woman's tone at the other end of the phone sounded wrong. He couldn't put a finger on it, but something wasn't right. He rolled up and out of bed and left the room, the chill of the air waking up his tired brain.

"Go ahead." He wondered if Sanctuary Ops was passing on an update from Dale. It had been days since his Sanctuary partner had been assigned the task of investigating this case.

"There's been an attempt on Gareth Headley's life while in custody." She cut to the chase so quick it took a few seconds for Nik's brain to catch up with the words. "Just wanted to give you the heads-up that Dale says he is getting closer to the source of all this." Okay, good, next Nik needed to know Morgan would be safe.

"Is this going to have an impact on us here?"

"The leak isn't in Sanctuary, so nothing leaves this room on your location. The leak is definitely fed based." *Jeez, how clichéd can this get?* "Keep your eyes open, and look after your boy. If they reached out to get to the cop inside then they're sure to have your boy on their list next."

"Okay." What else could he say? Morgan was in danger, hence Nik having him in protective custody and the reason for his job. The nebulous "bad guys" were clearly intent on eliminating evidence trails with both Morgan and the cop.

"Oh and Nikolai? With the new data Dale is providing, there is evidence of a definite link to the Bullen family."

Organized crime, Nik thought immediately, *not good, really not good.*

Ops continued, "There are some back links to the Bullen campaign for governor. The FBI's Organized Crime Unit is making noises about having Morgan back under their auspices—"

"Not going to happen," Nik growled.

"Which is what Jake said you would say, so the feds got the message." Jake, as owner and director of Sanctuary, was always one hundred percent behind his operatives. Nik didn't even begin to question the anxiety that coiled in him at the thought of Morgan being taken from his control. She ended the call with an assurance Dale's reports were copied to Morgan's master file and a brusque goodbye.

For a while he stood where he had ended up, the office in the attic, as naked as the day he was born, looking out of the barred window to the water beyond. The FBI wanted Morgan back? That wasn't going to happen any time soon, not if Dale was convinced a single fed was somehow touched with the stain of organized crime or linked to the corruption that tainted the Bullen campaign for governor. Bullen, the eldest son of an eldest son, was the stuff of newspaper front pages. In his fifties, rich, and clever, he'd been backed to rise as far as it was possible to rise in the murky world of politics. Rumor had him connected to the dirtier side of the Bullen family. There was nothing more than unsubstantiated anecdotes by people who had dealt with the Bullens. No one would come forward with anything concrete, but the rumours and the anonymous tips were enough to have the man watched.

He wasn't sure why his first thought was to feel sorry for Morgan or why it made him so sad to see the man who had gotten so under his skin involved in this shit. From being in the wrong place at the wrong time to ending up in the ass-end of nowhere wasn't exactly a fair deal in life.

Strong hands slid around him, and Nik berated himself for not hearing Morgan climb the stairs. Morgan was still warm from bed, his hands strong and firm in their hold around his waist and across his stomach. Nik groaned inwardly as his dick showed an interest in the company of a sleepy Morgan.

"What did they say to you?"

"Nothing." Damn it, that wasn't what he meant to say. He leaned into Morgan's hold, the cell phone gripped tight in his hand. "And everything."

"Talk to me." Morgan's voice still held a half asleep grumble.

"There was an attempt on Gareth Headley's life in prison." Morgan didn't reply, and apart from his tightening his hold on Nik, it would seem he hadn't even heard. "I would lay twenty on the fact, with you still alive and able to testify against Gareth, they decided to get him out of the way instead." He moved out of Morgan's hold, turning to face him. "I need coffee." He looked at Morgan where he stood in sweats and little else. "And clothes. You put the coffee on."

Ten minutes later, dressed, warmer, and a little less rattled, Nik took his seat at the wooden table and sipped on the hot coffee. He knew he needed to explain more about what the hell was going on, but he wasn't sure he even knew where to start.

"I don't understand…" Morgan dropped into the chair beside him and leaned close. "I mean… I do understand why, but I don't see…" He huffed a small sound of resignation, a warm puff of air on Nik's shoulder.

Nik owed him some kind of explanation. Keeping his thoughts to himself and leaving Morgan in the dark wasn't the right thing to do.

"I'm guessing, and I haven't looked at Dale's report so this is conjecture from Ops. If you are removed from the picture then you can't testify against him and he walks free. Otherwise, and this could be easier for the perps, the cop dies so he can't talk. Full stop."

"He hasn't talked up to now."

"Maybe he thought he wouldn't need to cut a deal, if you were dead."

"And when they didn't succeed in killing me, he probably got scared. Maybe he even threatened to talk." Morgan sounded so matter-of-fact, and Nik watched carefully for any cracks in the calm accepting tone.

"Exactly," he stated. "Headley threatening to talk, and them failing to kill you, leads to a shiv in the stomach." Morgan winced, and Nik immediately regretted the harsh words.

"Is it what they did? Stabbed him in the gut?" Morgan dropped his hands and covered his own stomach. Nik contemplated softening it, lying, but at the end of the day, it was something better out than in.

"It's the usual way people get hurt in prison, an easy weapon—"

"Do they know who did it?" Morgan frowned as he asked the question. Nik could see the other man's thought processes clear as day written in the half scowl on his face.

"I don't know any more yet, but they'll send what they know when they can," he offered gently, and then aborted his attempt to grasp Morgan by the hand and reassure the man he was safe. He didn't want to pull this down to the level of attraction. The rest of their time together had to be bodyguard/client or nothing at all. Morgan stared into his coffee, and Nik wished he could hear what was going through the man's thoughts. He didn't have to wait for long. He had realized a few days before if Morgan thought something then he needed to verbalize it.

"What was the girl in the alleyway involved in for god's sake?"

And *there* was the million dollar question.

Chapter Ten

THE DAY HAD BEEN QUIET. MORGAN SEEMED LOST IN
thought and had made himself comfortable on the jetty
with sketch pad in hand. Nik had found some more
pencils and even a child's tin of poster paints. Morgan
had hoarded the treasures in a plastic box and had taken
the whole lot outside with determination in his stride. He
didn't appear to need company, and even after the
physical stuff they had done the night before, Nik didn't
feel like he should interrupt. He took out coffee at
regular intervals and found ground beef at the back of
the huge walk-in freezer. After cooking burgers, he
watched from his usual spot between the two trees to
make sure Morgan ate the food, trying to gauge how the
other man felt.

Morgan probably had an awful lot to think about
with the stark reminder of the death threat. He was
sketching furiously on the pad with the colored pencils,
every so often looking up to the sky. It gave the
impression he wasn't drawing a still life image from

what he could see but rather creating something from his own memories. Nik wanted to look, to crouch down next to Morgan and ask to see what had the younger man looking so intensely involved. On the other hand, Morgan was clearly engrossed, and when he was ready, he could certainly come over to Nik if he wanted to talk.

Nik found himself doing a lot of thinking also. That was the good thing about this job; when there was downtime, there was *downtime*. He had come close in his head to regretting what they had done last night, in the shower, in the bedroom, wondering if it really had been a good idea given the updated situation. It had been hot, intense and he'd never had such a responsive lover writhing under him or such a giving partner when the roles were reversed. Of course he would meet the first man to make everything seem easy in the middle of a murder trial. He shuffled the paperwork on his lap and connected to Ops via his satellite phone. The scrambled transmission was quick and to the point.

"How close is Dale to the core of this case?" he asked, watching as Morgan looked towards him at the sound of his voice.

"Close enough, and trial is still set for the fifteenth."

"I need to be doing something, financials to trawl through, evidence to sift, anything."

"We can do that, but—" She sighed, irritation in the sound. "—this isn't coming from me, Nikolai, Sanctuary brass is fighting this, but the feds are still pushing for Morgan to be returned to them and have demanded your position."

"If they—"

"They won't, and if there was anything, there would be a heads-up for you. We need you to keep the client on the down low, and if he thinks of anything pertaining to the case, we need to know."

"He didn't even know the woman in the alley, let alone have any idea why the cop killed her."

"We are aware of that."

"Morgan knows nothing else that can help."

"You appear convinced. Do you know something we don't, Nikolai?" Her voice had softened. He had a good relationship with Ops, and they generally listened to what his instincts told him. Thing is, every single one of them was also too damned intuitive, and if he opened his mouth to say any more, they would probably put two and two together and realize he had broken all the rules.

"No," he said simply. With a few last pieces of information and some new codes for the files, they ended the call.

He caught movement out of the corner of his eye, a flash of brown in the reeds at the edge of the water, and he realized it was an otter. He didn't move. It was closer to him than it was to Morgan, and all he wanted to do was call over and tell the other man. If he did that, it would swim off. Carefully he settled the papers to one side, and cautiously, quietly, he moved towards Morgan, who looked up at him when he sensed the approach.

"Look," he whispered and pointed where the otter had been. There wasn't anything there, and he squinted into the sun, trying to get a handle on any movement. Morgan stood and leaned into him so he could see, but there was nothing for him to see. Disappointment washed through Nik. He had never seen an otter in the wild, but when there was a quiet barely there "look" from Morgan, he saw the timid creature again, and for minutes, the two of them stood frozen, quietly watching. Morgan's hand slipped into his, the sun was high in the sky, the breeze was cooling, and there were only the gentle sounds of rippling water and the wind in the trees to break the absolute peace.

The otter raised its snout and scented the air, and then in a flash, it was under the water and away.

"Did you know there were otters here?" Nik said softly, not wanting to ruin the peace.

"I saw some evidence of it when I was in the lake yesterday." Nik didn't want to remember yesterday and the image of Morgan clambering up onto the grass, a wide grin on his face and water sheeting from him. Nik had been hard in seconds, and that was before he knew what the skin under the clothes tasted like. If Morgan went swimming this morning, he wasn't sure he would be able to keep himself from drooling.

"I've never seen an otter up close," Nik said softly.

"Neither have I, not actually in a lake, in its home."

Nik closed his arms around Morgan, allowing him to lean back, and they simply stood there looking out over the water, Nik imagining this huge network of whatever otters called their homes.

"What was the call about?"

Nik tensed; he should have known Morgan would ask.

He tried really hard to keep a normal tone. "Some tech stuff. Really nothing new."

"Okay." Morgan appeared happy to accept what he was saying, and in fact, he turned in Nik's arms and looped one hand around Nik's neck, pulling him down for a gentle kiss. Morgan asked for more with a touch of his tongue to the seam of Nik's lips, and Nik didn't have any defense, deepening the kiss on a sigh. When Morgan pulled back, he had a worried look on his face.

"I'm sorry I went all stupid and worried today. It's hard to make sense of how I feel about what I saw and what she may have been involved in. But I don't want to add to the stress levels around here."

"You were scared and seemed kind of sad. It makes sense to internalize it to get your thoughts straight."

"I'm still scared."

Nik simply buried his face into the juncture of Morgan's neck and shoulder, not trusting himself to tell Morgan that he was scared as well. Scared he would fail Morgan. Fail at this assignment. Morgan was slowly and surely showing him how things could be if only he let himself enjoy what was offered. It wasn't possible love was what they had so early on. Surely it was really a simple proximity-driven lust gentled with an ounce of affection. But this artist who sat and drew intricate scenes intrigued him. There was so much about Morgan Nik wanted to know and questions he needed to ask himself, not least of which was the thought that Morgan had been the thing missing from his life for far too long. He needed to get perspective.

Being with Morgan was a nice place to be, fun, and a break from real life for just a few days. The fear that clenched his stomach didn't necessarily mean what he felt couldn't be sustained past the trial. If the authorities told Morgan it wasn't safe to stay in New York State, then Morgan was right. He would probably have to move away. It was unlikely they would see each other again, let alone experience this passion they had for each other after the trial date.

"Want to go for a swim?" Morgan asked him for probably the hundredth time since they'd found the water. He thought briefly on the reasons why he couldn't swim and realized none of them mattered at the moment. They could go back and lock away the Glock. They could even search out swim shorts if they felt like it.

"Okay."

Once in the water, it became clear that swimming was really Morgan's thing, though Nik did give as good as he got. As he pointed out, he did come a close second in the race to the other side and back again. Neither worried about swim shorts, and the cold water kept things cooled. There was simply laughter and fun, and a moment Nik thought he might well remember for a long time.

Swimming led to kissing and, on the bank, groping, which resulted in a splinter in Nik's left butt cheek and his knee throbbing like a bitch. Together they limped and stumbled back to the cabin, and Nik entered the code for lockdown. He knew where this was heading.

"You should have said something if your knee was hurting. I climbed all over you."

"Yeah, which was nice," Nik teased, and Morgan punched him on the arm.

"Ass."

"It doesn't hurt much now, and even when it does, I'm used to it. I have meds; it'll be fine."

"And you say the splinter went…" Morgan couldn't seem to help the laugh that tumbled from him as he waved in the general area of Nik's backside.

"You can laugh, but it's you pulling it out." Morgan proceeded to help out, getting Nik to lean over the side of the sofa so he could finagle the offending piece of deck out of Nik's ass. But hell if the idiot could stop laughing as he did it.

"You going to stop laughing? Or do I have to make you stop?" Nik looked back over his shoulder to see Morgan stifle his laugh.

"Big bad bodyguard has an ouchy," Morgan sing-songed with a grin and a wicked gleam in his blue eyes. He took a step back, and the laughter that bubbled from him was uncontrolled and beautiful. He collapsed to the floor and lay back on the rug, and Nik followed him. His hands pinned, his legs caught between Nik's, Morgan started to laugh again.

Nik struggled not to join in. Morgan's laugh was so damn infectious, like a kid's giggle. Not only that, but in laughing Morgan had thrown his head back. His neck was exposed, laid bare, from throat to lips. Nik lowered his mouth and started to kiss. He concentrated on the pulse at the base of Morgan's throat, feeling it flutter against his cool lips. Darting out his tongue and tasting the taut skin, he listened as Morgan's laughter turned slowly to soft whimpers and whispers of his name… Nikolai, Nik.

Nik started to explore higher, kiss-biting a path up

the side of Morgan's neck, shifting his body slightly as his hard dick pressed against Morgan's, so fucking turned on for this man imprisoned under him. He didn't let go of Morgan's hands as he pushed down, aligning himself, desperate to make a memory with Morgan today.

He could feel Morgan hot and hard against him, and he moved subtly, pushing his own sex against the younger man's, reaching up to swallow Morgan's resulting groan with an open-mouthed kiss. He swallowed his name from Morgan's lips, tongues meeting, tasting, hard and insistent, slanting his head to reach deeper inside. Releasing Morgan's hands, he felt them instantly move to dig deep into his hair, pulling and twisting into the damp length of it. Morgan was arching up into the kiss. Nik heard himself groan, pushing up and away slightly, not taking his lips from Morgan's, just reaching between them to palm Morgan's dick. Morgan groaned and whimpered into Nik's mouth, wrenching his lips away to say one word, "Please." The sound was caught somewhere between a plea and a demand.

Nik didn't hesitate, didn't argue. He pulled their dicks together in one hand, hot, heavy, hard, twisting, and captured Morgan's mouth in a kiss that stole Nik's breath. They moved unevenly, desperately, intent on only one thing. A singular twist of Morgan's hips against Nik's hand, and Morgan was lost, shouting his completion and arching so hard he smacked his head back on the floor. Nik felt the tension, the iron grip, the release, the heat, the intensity of Morgan's bliss and fell over the edge himself, hot against the writhing man.

They stayed still, breathing hard, neither moving to break the intense hold the experience had created until Morgan twisted a leg, using momentum and surprise to push Nik onto his back and lean over him to capture his kiss-bitten lips with a soft touch.

"It wasn't a very big splinter, you know," he murmured. Laughter was creeping back into his voice.

"It was a plank," Nik said in defense.

"We need to get up off of the floor."

"No, Morgan. We don't."

Chapter Eleven

THIS TIME THE CALL HAPPENED AT 8:07 IN THE morning, and when Nik stretched to reach the phone, he realized Morgan wasn't in bed with him. He answered the call and swung his feet to the floor, stretching his muscles and yawning widely. Instinct had him glancing at the windows and seeing them locked and barred. At least Morgan had kept lockdown in place.

"Hey," he responded to a wide awake operative who got straight to the point.

"Dale and the cops made arrests last night. Not high enough up the food chain to implicate Bullen and his run for governor, although way past enough to get to the prison hospital where Gareth Headley is being kept and to put the pressure on him. If Headley knows there are others who could potentially reveal links to what name he is hiding, it's in his best interest to talk first." Nik digested the succinct information and filtered it through three depths of sleep. Arrests, Bullen, Headley, prison.

"Do you think he'll actually break?" he finally asked,

shaking his head to clear the cobwebs. He was usually an up-and-at 'em early riser, but he enjoyed being wrapped around Morgan so much he found it harder and harder to get out of bed in the morning. Still, Morgan wasn't here now so he concentrated on what he was being told. He wasn't going to go soft under the influence of good sex.

"He's a cop on remand for being a killer," Ops responded drily. "The death penalty is under a court-ordered moratorium, but for sure it's life without parole. Enough leverage and Dale may get Headley to give us something useful." She sounded hopeful, and it was enough to send a frisson of near-relief running through him. Headley revealing who he worked for would allow the authorities to remove that person from the equation and maybe lift the threat to Morgan. Which was *good* news in amongst a whole load of what-ifs.

When the call was over, he went off to find his new lover, which wasn't hard, considering the small space and the few rooms. He located Morgan finally in the front room, sprawled, legs and arms akimbo on the sofa. A blanket was up to his chin and covered about two thirds of his body, forming a barrier between the cool air and any possible nakedness. His breathing was steady and even, bordering every so often on a small snore and a cute kind of sniffle. Nik stood and watched for a long time, leaning against the door frame and crossing his arms. Torn between wanting to wake Morgan and wanting to watch him sleep, he debated the pros and cons. On the pro side for waking him up, there were obvious benefits. Kissing, making out, touching, orgasms, laughter and so much more. On the con side, he couldn't find any for the list, but damn it, he couldn't justify waking Morgan—he looked so innocent lying there. Nik smirked at his thoughts. Innocent with a side of cute and sleepy and fucking sexy.

"You're staring…" Morgan's voice had a sexy growl to it. His dark hair was in disarray and his yawn wide. Nik straightened and felt heat rise in his cheeks that he had been caught gawking like a girl. A thousand and one witty comebacks were usually at his disposal, but none of them came to mind after his phone conversation with Ops.

"Coffee?" was the only thing he could manage as he crossed to the counter. Coffee was the only way to start the day. When he heard the chair scrape, he pictured Morgan sitting at the table, sweats low on his hips, and jeez, did his dick sit up and take notice of *that* image. "More dreams?" he asked.

"Hmmm?"

Nik placed coffee in front of Morgan and slid into the chair opposite. "You were up early. Was it the dreams again?"

"Nah." He ran hands through his already spiky hair and frowned. "You stole the covers, and I was cold."

Which was so not what Nik expected to hear, and an explosive snort of laughter escaped from him at the woebegone expression Morgan had on his face. "Why didn't you take some back?" he asked curiously.

"I did, but your huge-assed heaviness was holding them down, and then you got cross."

"Cross?"

"Yep, in your sleep, muttering something about guns. I thought it best to back off." Morgan blew on the coffee and took a swallow, half closing his eyes and then making this damn sexy, half-purring sigh. Nik squirmed in his chair, not wanting to be obvious about repositioning his dick, which was tenting his sweats.

"Why didn't you use another bedroom?" he asked.

Morgan shrugged. "Didn't think of that."

"Wanna go back to bed for an hour, get warm?" Nik leaned in to steal a kiss.

Morgan smiled into the kiss then tilted his head in contemplation. "Then a swim?"

God, he was nothing if not persistent. "Then a swim I guess," Nik agreed, shivering at the thought of the near icy water this early in the day. Coffees in hand, they went back into the main bedroom. Morgan hadn't been lying. Nik could see the quilt pooled on the floor on his side and the other half over his pillows, leaving nothing for his Morgan.

"My bad," he apologized quickly, and then scrambled up the bed, the chill of the morning air requiring a quilt around his ears as soon as possible. Morgan climbed in more sedately, waiting, clearly, for Nik to push over more quilt. He did, but at the same time, he grabbed a handful of wriggling, near-on giggling, ticklish lover and pulled him in to spoon him from behind. They lay close together, Nik cupping Morgan with one hand trapped beneath his muscled back, skin on skin.

"Caveman," Morgan snapped. Then belying any irritation, he pushed his butt back against Nik's groin. He felt so good, and unerringly, Nik wrapped his free hand around his lover's morning wood, twisting at the tip of the heat and loving the way Morgan snuggled in. He could fall asleep like this, wrapped around this man, inhaling the warm sleepy scent of him.

"Are you going to do anything with what you got hold of, bodyguard? Enquiring minds and all that."

"I might..." He moved his hand again, the warmth of soft skin against his fingertips, Morgan's strength under his control. Morgan muttered something under his breath, something that sounded suspiciously like "I'll fall asleep if you don't get a move on." Half of him wanted to tease and prolong it; the other half was desperate for another taste. It was the latter half that won.

Chapter Twelve

DAYS RAN LIKE MOLASSES, SLOW AND STEADY AND filled with enough memories for Morgan to take away with him. Three days to trial, and the tension ramped up. Nik had become super-vigilant-bodyguard-man which made for an uneasy "treading on eggshells" type of atmosphere. There were phone calls back and forth, and his lover spent a lot of time on the computer accessing files and planning routes to the court. Dale was coming out to assist the transfer. Three hours from here to there and it would all be over. They walked around the back of the cabin and found the small path that took them to a widened clearing, empty of weeds and circular in shape.

"What is this for?"

"Helicopter," Nik said with the air of someone who talked about such things every day.

"This is a helicopter landing area?" Morgan attempted to swallow equal parts of amazement and utter terror. Nik turned around and frowned.

"It is. How else do you think we are going to get you to the city for the trial?"

Shit. Not by air. There was a reason he hadn't ever been far out of New York State. "Ummm, same way we got here?" he offered carefully.

"Impossible, too many variables—"

"Jeez, Nik, I read books and watch movies, you know. Helicopters crash."

"Cars crash."

"Not from a great height." Morgan tried not to sound like the wuss he was, but really heights were not his thing, and flying in a *plane* was way off his radar. Strapping himself into a helicopter and free-wheeling out of this tiny space into the heavens sent fear spiraling through him. Nik drew him into a close hug.

"I'll look after you."

"You say that now." His voice was muffled against Nik's broad chest, and not for the first time, he felt like this short girl-guy who needed protection. "What if the pilot has a heart attack when he's flying?"

"I'll be on the flight with you; I'll take over."

"You can fly a helicopter?"

"Well, I know enough." *Of course you do,* Morgan thought wryly, but didn't say the words.

"Why doesn't this surprise me?" Morgan finally muttered, burying into Nik's hold and clinging for dear life. "I'm guessing it's a prerequisite for all ninja bodyguards to be able to fly an aircraft." It was a rhetorical question, and laughter vibrated in Nik.

———

TWO DAYS TO go and Morgan didn't want to leave bed. He had long since caught up on sleep and now all he wanted was tasting and touching and Nik pasted all over him. He had never had an experience like it. Nik was an attentive, strong, focused lover who never failed to make Morgan see stars. It was a whole new experience to have a lover who actually made an effort to get him off as well as himself. Intense feelings wound themselves around his body, and damn it, his heart wasn't unaffected.

Maybe it was fear that his permanent safety would mean he would never see Nik again, maybe it was fear for his life? Whatever it was driving him, he couldn't let Nik out of his sight. He followed Nik everywhere, only drawing a line at following him into the toilet. To his credit, Nik was laid back about it for a while, and then suddenly he wasn't.

"Will. You. Quit. Following. Me," he stated carefully, emphasizing syllables and, in general, conveying the irritation Morgan knew he must be feeling.

"I can't." Well, at least he was being honest and up front. Surely Nik had to take this into consideration and allow Morgan a few moments of neediness.

He didn't.

"Well, you have to. I can't think. You are driving me mad."

"Oh." There wasn't a lot else he could say to that one. His honesty had led to Nik feeling he could be just as blunt. With an irritated huff, Nik took a few steps towards the front door, and in a synchronized movement, Morgan took the same two steps.

"Stop it!" Nik underlined his frustration by the heavy use of a firm palm-out hand in front of him. "I need to think, and I can't stand you near me. If we don't get this transfer right then we leave you vulnerable."

"Sorry." Morgan tried for meek, but realized as he said it he had perhaps allowed too much sarcasm to slip into the tone. Nik's expression went from exasperated to angry in a second.

"Do you want to die?" he snapped then with an unceremonious shove, he pushed Morgan back against the wall and stalked off into the sunlight in the yard beyond. Cabin fever was getting to them both, but two weeks of not talking about how he felt, of letting it fester under his skin meant there was a lot of poison in his head to bubble to the surface. He closed his eyes as a wave of misery swallowed him whole, and the start of a panic attack began to tear at the edges of his control.

"No," he shouted, nearly screamed, after the retreating Nik, who stopped and turned in a sudden stop-start flurry of motion. Through his cloud of emotions, he saw Nik with his hand on his weapon, clearly thinking Morgan was in danger, and there was the icing on the cake. "I don't want to die. I didn't want to see that woman lose her face in front of me. I don't want to give evidence. I don't want anything to do with this. I don't want to never see you again after the trial." Where had that come from? Morgan stopped, holding himself upright with a hand to the door frame, and Nik didn't move. He simply held out a hand.

"Come on, let's sit," he offered in a tone of voice Morgan hadn't heard before, firm and unyielding. More like the bodyguard he had first met. All business.

"What if I don't want to..." *Childish much?*

"Come on."

He sighed and crossed to where Nik stood, taking the offered hand in a death grip and then let himself be led to the jetty, climbing the timbers until they sat next to each other, their feet dangling over the edge of the dock, mere inches above the clear water below.

"As your bodyguard, I need to be here for you and keep you from getting killed. You understand this, right?" Nik sounded hesitant as he asked the question.

"I know," Morgan replied quickly, "and I don't mean to get in your way."

"You aren't—god... it isn't that you get in my way. I have this whole set of scenarios in my head, and my head... it's a scary place. Then there you are, standing next to me, and all I can do is smell you and know you are alive." He exhaled noisily.

"Nik?" Morgan couldn't read anything in the tone of Nik's voice.

"We could, you know, not even go to the court. We could hide." Nik sounded suddenly so eager, like he had offered the answer to everything in that one sentence.

"What?"

"It's something that's been running through my head. Why am I even doing this? Why am I taking you straight back to where you could get hurt, and then letting you disappear into nowhere?"

"Because it's your job."

Nik threw a stone into the water, the ripples spreading and reaching the shore, and Morgan was transfixed, both by the motion of the water and the words Nik had spoken.

"If I said yes?" he began carefully. "Nik, if I agreed, and we went and hid somewhere, you wouldn't think much of me as a man."

"It wouldn't matter what I thought. At least you'd be safe."

"Nik—"

"I know, okay?" Morgan waited for the rest of the sentence, twisting his fingers around Nik's and gripping tight. "I'm not good at this."

"You and me both."

"I don't want you to be scared, or hurt, or have to go off to fuck knows where so I never get to see you again. I want to come off assignments with Sanctuary and use my two-week furloughs to go home to you."

"You do?" Morgan heard the surprise in his voice. It all sounded very domestic and, he had to be honest with himself, appealing.

"Does that sound creepy? Is it…" Again Nik paused, clearly struggling to find words. "Is this some crazy Stockholm syndrome shit? Do you feel…? Look, is it too soon to make the decision to want?"

"Want what?"

"All of it. The coming home to you, the memories, and something real?"

"No." Morgan leaned into Nik's warmth, choosing his words carefully. "It's been two weeks. My parents met and married in a little over three weeks."

"Married?"

"Yep, happy until the day my Dad died, so I don't think there is a time limit on how quickly you can fall in love." Nik twisted where he sat, causing Morgan to slip farther to the side, and then caught him in a hard hold, hands around his upper arms.

"Love?" he demanded quickly. "You think what is happening here is love?"

Morgan frowned at the words, spoken so quickly and with such urgency. *Isn't that what we have been talking about?* Best to get the fact out there. "Umm... yeah... that is what I'm talking about."

Nik bowed his head, almost curled in on himself, but still with the bruising grip on Morgan's arms. When he raised his head, there was utter determination in his expression, and he smiled grimly.

"I love you, Morgan Drake, and I am not losing you to a bullet. Understand? "

"I don't want to throw a wrench in the works, but what about—"

"No." Nik's voice was strident, and Morgan stopped talking immediately. "No more talking or over-thinking." He released his hold on Morgan and scrambled to stand. Holding out his left hand so he could help Morgan up, mentally he was already thumbing through his contacts and making his selection.

"You know I probably love you, too," Morgan said simply, realizing he hadn't even vocalized how he actually felt as his take-charge lover did what he did best—took charge. Nik smiled at the words and opened his mouth to say something, but stopped when whoever he had called answered, and suddenly he was all business.

"Dale, how close are you now?"

Morgan unashamedly listened to Nik's side of the conversation and then waited patiently for a summary. Nik was quick to offer the report.

"Dale has had contact with the DA's office. They're working the case from that end, trying to get Headley to talk." Nik didn't immediately launch into a promise the DA's office was arranging things, or that Dale's contact had managed to get Headley's cooperation. In fact, he looked troubled. Half of Morgan wanted to ask what was wrong; the other half wanted blissful ignorance. It was a need to know that finally pushed him to ask a question.

"And?"

"Headley's defense lawyer is playing games. Dale says it's some of the more usual delaying tactics."

"Like?"

"Calling on any slight errors in the chain of evidence like the retrieval, blood splatters, other forensics. When it comes down to it, your evidence is crucial. They can't discredit what you saw. Also the judge is refusing to push back the trial date."

"That's a good thing, right? Anything to get this over and done with." Even as he said the words he wanted to recall them. Was it wrong to want to stay here in the middle of freaking nowhere with Nik and never actually leave?

Chapter Thirteen

FROM SLOW DAYS, THE END CAME SO DAMN SUDDENLY, with the alarm on Nik's satellite phone dragging Morgan from a deep and blessedly dreamless sleep. It seemed only yesterday they had looked at the clearing where the helicopter would land, talking about going to the city, and now two days later, the day to go was here. Nik wasn't under the covers with him. He was probably already showered, dressed, and doing final checks. When Morgan found him, there were no words exchanged, simply gentle kisses, the time for final passion and touches long past. They had said their goodbyes the night before, and Morgan would remember every single word, kiss, and movement for the rest of his natural life.

Whatever happened, according to Dale's information feeds to Nik, it seemed the federal government had decided Morgan wasn't a candidate for full witness protection. The reasoning behind it fell mostly to the fact they had bigger fish to fry. Morgan knew nothing apart from the identity of the shooter, and that meant he was of no further use. After Nik had gotten deeper into a call last night, citing the attempt on Morgan's life and getting himself into an emotional tailspin, Dale had said something that had finally got through the upended feelings and left Nik looking ill.

"What did he say?"

"That, at the end of the day, it's either you or the cop. It's nothing we didn't already think. Whoever is behind this, there is no way in holy hell they will either let you testify or let the cop talk. If you are alive, you can get him convicted, and there will be the chance that, faced with the reality of prison, Headley will turn state's evidence in order to get some kind of lesser sentence."

"They have those others though. Dale, your friend, found links higher up to the organized crime and the politician. Doesn't that information make me kind of insignificant now?"

It was a valid point, but Morgan wasn't convinced Nik was agreeing with what he was saying. He seemed in a world of his own, making several more calls Morgan wasn't privy to. Finally the moment arrived, and the helicopter with the pilot and another man was there. The tall, blond, scary one was clearly Dale.

Dale, who wouldn't actually look him in the eye. He just went about business with the scary protector-type stuff Nik made look so effortless. There were guns, and plans, and talking in code. Morgan ended up taking himself away from the two men and waiting until Nik locked down Sanctuary Seven.

The noise of the blades was raucous in the quiet

forest. How could the Sanctuary Foundation even think for one moment the copter wouldn't be noticed by *someone*? With his eyes shut for the first movement of the silver bird, they rose into the air.

"Look." Nik's voice was faint through the headphones they were all wearing, and it wasn't exactly the quietest of environments. Gripping Nik's hand, Morgan opened his eyes, his stomach lurching and his meager breakfast threatening to return. Then he saw what Nik was pointing at. Their cabin, the lake an almost perfect oval off to one side, the old wooden jumble of jetty. The water looked stunning from the air, but the cabin faded to nothing, hidden almost immediately in the canopy of trees. All that was left was the rough looking circle of cleared ground where the helicopter had sat, and even that blurred into the landscape after a few seconds. Even more so as the helicopter turned away south onwards to whatever would face them all.

The loss of what he could see, and the memories he and Nik had made, dug deep into him until it was nearly impossible to breathe. Nik must have noticed his distress. He did nothing more than grip his hand, but it was enough for Morgan to focus on.

———

DALE LED them from the helipad, his eyes trained ahead. It seemed Nik was simply intent on crowding Morgan as much as he could, until finally they were into the stairwell on floor twenty-three of the stately Hotel Grande. They made it to the seventeenth floor before

Dale deemed it safe to use the service elevator. He didn't say much, this protector, even though Morgan was brimming with questions he wanted answered. Who had Dale tracked down, what exactly had the victim been involved in, why did Headley shoot her? He kept quiet though because he didn't want to interrupt either Dale's or Nik's utter focus. Both had weapons drawn as the elevator doors opened in the basement, and they remained drawn until they made it through the kitchen to the back door.

"Maybe I should have a gun, guys?" he said as they reached the outside, and he looked around nervously. They were two minutes from the courthouse and, not for the first time, he wondered why, in the city of possible assailants, he was the only one unarmed. It was different from the cabin, noisy, complicated and scary, and to his mind, there could be a man on every roof with a rifle trained at his heart. He even looked down at his chest for the telltale red dot of a gun aimed on him, brushing the front of his shirt absently.

"You don't need a gun," Nik said softly, moving to crowd Morgan without, it seemed, making it too obvious.

"What if—"

"Shhh, stop talking," Dale hissed, and Morgan subsided into silence, wondering exactly why he had to be quiet in the city. It didn't last long.

"Shouldn't I have a bulletproof vest, or some kind of armored vehicle?"

"Subtle, Drake, we want subtle," Dale snarled in return. "Now shut up."

They reached the wide steps leading to the courthouse, a mountain of worn pale-colored stone and a thousand feet moving along and up and down. Morgan didn't even want to mention a possible back door entry, clearly going in the front door was a confusion tactic, if the bad guys expected them to go in the back way. Wait though... What if the bad guys thought of this too, and decided it was exactly what an ex-fed would do, and this meant they had their sights aimed at him now?

"Stop thinking." Nik knocked arms with him and smiled at him briefly.

Jeez. *Stop talking? Stop thinking? I might as well stop breathing.* Shit. Actually passing into the courthouse was anticlimactic. He didn't know what he'd expected, but the quiet and courteous patdown he received wasn't it. Nik and Dale handed over weapons and entered codes into secure lockboxes and were patted down one at a time, each with a careful eye on Morgan. Finally all three of them were led to a small room off the main corridor. Morgan sat himself in one corner, bolt upright, hands in his lap, and anxiety in the pit of his stomach. His throat felt tight and his eyes itchy, so he closed his eyes, focused on the cool, nearly cold, water of Lake Dante, the cabin, the trees, and Nik. He repeated it on a loop, each memory better and clearer than the last until finally he could feel the tension inside him loosen.

When he opened his eyes, it was to see Nik sitting opposite with a carefully placed mask on his face. There was no sign of the lover who clung to him in the dark in the closed expression and certainly no glimpse of the worry or fear he'd revealed when they sat by the lake.

This was Nik the bodyguard, and it was reassuring. Dale, on the other hand, was pacing, his cell in his hand and a frown creasing his brow.

"This is stupid," he finally announced to Morgan and Nik.

"What?" Morgan was curious as to how the trial could be labeled stupid.

"Nothing."

"Dale?" This came from Nik, whose expression was now a lot more open.

"She should have—Jeez—"

"Is this something to do with the DA?"

"I called in favors is all, pulled some strings, wanted to get Headley to turn before this goes any further." Morgan's stomach lurched, and then he started violently when the door banged open against the wall, and a tall lady in a suit walked in. Nik stood in front of Morgan in a flash, and Dale was a barrier to both of them. It was an impasse; no one seemed to know what to say to the beautiful woman who had walked in. Then Dale took a step forward.

"And?"

The woman smiled and nodded, and with a whoop, Dale swung her high in the air.

"Put me down, you idiot." She half laughed.

He set her down, and she straightened her tailored suit.

"He rolled?" Dale questioned.

"Turned state's evidence," she responded quickly.

"What?" Morgan wasn't following this, the hope inside him a very small flame. This was too easy.

The woman continued, "Headley has turned state's evidence and pled guilty to the murder of Elisabeth Costain. It isn't clear what the Bullens had over Headley to have him in their pockets. We don't know full details as yet. We moved the wife and kids, promised them protection, and he rolled. On Bullen, it's a big case."

Morgan had questions. "Do I have to—" The woman held up a hand to silence him.

"There'll be no trial for him. He'll go straight to sentencing after depositions," she began carefully then reached to pull the door shut on all four of them. "My brother here led us on a very profitable trail for contacts." Morgan nodded, the words buzzing in his head. Dale and the woman were siblings. They looked alike—both tall and blond—and he definitely saw some family resemblance.

"Thank you," Nik was saying, and he added more as he shook Dale's hand and kissed the sister prettily on the cheek. The woman was clearly some kind of court official or a lawyer or something, and he couldn't believe what everyone was saying. "I don't know who you are." *Jeez, that sounded so rude.*

"Lissa MacIntyre, DA's Office. Dale gave us enough links to pull Headley out of the mire." Morgan listened to the words, but he had more questions. Why did Elisabeth have to die in that alley?

"Why?" In his dreams, he'd asked the cop, the one with the gun on his victim, the one who chased him when Morgan literally ran for his life, several questions: Why did you shoot her? What did she do? What did she do that was so bad she had to die? They stopped talking, and Nik looked directly at him.

"You won't need to testify."

"No. I need to know… In my dream, I always asked him why he had to shoot Elisabeth. What made him shoot her?"

"It isn't clear, Morgan," Lissa offered carefully. "It doesn't appear Headley knows why. He just felt he was left with no choice when ordered to do it."

"So we can ask him. It's over; he can tell us."

"I am not sure the full details will come out in the interviews."

"Tell me what he said." Morgan had ceased to care about social niceties. Lissa looked at Nik, then at Dale and sighed.

"He said nothing. From what Dale and I pieced together, the victim had an ex-boyfriend, one of the lesser Bullen family members. I imagine she threatened to expose some connection to organized crime during the campaign for governor. "

"So suddenly Headley is a murder weapon and Elisabeth is dead." All the energy that had sustained him so far today vanished from him in one go, leaving him in one great rush, and he slumped back onto the chair. Nik crouched next to him, his face creased in concern.

"It's over, Morgan," Nik said so quietly Morgan had to lean down to listen. "The heat is off you. You don't need to testify today, and there will eventually be no mileage in wanting you, or needing you, dead."

"Eventually?"

"If there was a hit ordered on you… You don't need

to worry though. I'm not leaving your side until this is all cleared." Morgan touched his forehead to Nik's, and they sat that way for a little while, not moving when Dale and his sister left.

"Are you hungry?" Nik sounded like his mom used to sound when eating three meals a day solved the ills of the world.

"I could drink coffee. Or maybe whisky and beer." A drink sounded nice right about now. Together they left the room and after collecting his weapon from the front they walked around the long corridor outside of security to the back exit. Nik did the usual checks, his weapon in hand, his face carved in stone. They left the courthouse, and the glass fire door swung shut behind them. Nik was still in protector mode, his eyes scanning the roofs overlooking the exit. They were a few steps away from the door, and Morgan heard a great clatter of sound behind them. He turned to see Dale pushing the door open, smiled at the other man then saw his mouth wide open shouting something. Then there was a confusion of noise and action, Nik diving to push him away, then a flash so close to him he face-planted in gravel. The pain was incredible, a burn, a fire so intense behind his eyes he realized it couldn't be all from gravel. There was blood in his mouth. It tasted metallic and had the texture of a thick milkshake over his teeth. Where had the blood come from? Nik lay across him, still as stone. The pain intensified. It helped to close his eyes, even though someone—was it Dale?—was shouting for him to keep his eyes open.

Nik? Nik!

Chapter Fourteen

NIK SIGNED THE LAST OF THE PAPERWORK, HIS FINAL active job for Sanctuary before he moved to Ops for at least the next few months. His second to final, actually. His actual last role was to accompany Dale to decommission Sanctuary Three. It was something he could do on his way out to New York where the Sanctuary offices were.

S3 was an older building, part of a complex of smaller cabins just outside the city, and it had been deemed unusable. Given the delicacy of the operation and the fact Nik wasn't taking cases until he healed, he seemed the right person for the job. Hence the two hours in the car with Dale and his incessant talking.

"So Morgan texted me. He's doing well. Left his job, took his savings, and got himself a late place in art college. He's got a puppy, a black lab, says it follows him everywhere."

It was easy to tune it out. All Nik had to do was draw the cloak of guilt closer around him, and he wouldn't hear any of it. It was his fault the shooter had gotten close enough to a position where he could get to Morgan. If it hadn't been for Dale at the door, causing Morgan to turn at the right moment... It didn't matter the bullet was a through-shot in Nik's shoulder and the velocity had been slowed. The same bullet had impacted Morgan's cheekbone. To this day Nik couldn't get it straight in his head that the shooter was tasked to kill, paid to kill, and it didn't matter to the shooter when Morgan was to die. The cop may well have rolled over and spilled his guts, but Morgan had still been a target. He had known that would happen. Why didn't he just keep them inside the courthouse for a short while more?

They had the gunman but no lead on the man behind the kill order. The shooter who had taken his chance with Morgan was no more than a kid with a gun pulled from a gang. He could give them nothing useful. Morgan had been torn from Nik, bleeding, and he couldn't even stand up to stop the paramedics. Despite leaving the hospital himself after one day and haunting the reception area, Nik hadn't had the balls to speak to the man he had let down.

"So the last text, you are going to laugh at this—"

"If you mention Morgan or his freaking dog one more time, I will rip your throat out," Nik growled as Dale took the turn off the main road to Sanctuary Three.

"I was only—"

"Don't. He's happy, great. Do I wanna hear about him? No."

"You're a fucking idiot, Nikolai. Morgan—Shit he *never* stops asking after you."

"He'll get over it." Morgan had to get over it, because Nik doubted he could ever face his lover again and not feel overwhelmed with feelings that he had failed him.

"It wasn't your fault."

"Yeah right."

"Why are you being such an asshole?"

"No more talking." Nik ended the conversation, and Dale subsided into a miserably heavy silence.

Sanctuary Three was beautiful, but it was no longer far enough off the beaten path. Inquisitive climbers and hikers had found it after a nearby waterfall was included in some treasure trove hunt. Clearly anyone who found it couldn't get in, nor did the outside really hint at what the inside held, but its existence was documented with a simple search on Google.

Nik stopped the engine and climbed down. This was a quick in and out. Check the place was deserted, check for anything left after the techs ripped out the guts of it, close it down. No more than a few hours' work.

"You go ahead, Nik. I need to check in."

It seemed reasonable, and Nik didn't see he had been fucked over until two things happened at once. The vehicle behind him revved and reversed back down the way it had come, and Morgan walked out of the cabin. Shit. Morgan looked so damn good.

"There isn't much left in there," Morgan stated confidently, and strode forward to meet Nik. He looked well and strong. The scar on the left side of his face was prominent but had faded some over the six weeks since the shooting had happened. Nik was speechless, beyond furious. He'd been manipulated, first by Sanctuary and then Dale. He couldn't look at the scar, couldn't look at Morgan. He turned on his heel, prepared to walk the odd mile or two back to the main road.

"Do you think you let him shoot me?" *That* stopped Nik in his tracks, and he spun back to face Morgan, incredulous shock slicing through him. He may well have failed at protecting his client, but he didn't *let* the guy shoot Morgan. Then, just as quickly, guilt overwhelmed him, guilt that told him Morgan was right. He had every reason to believe Nik would protect him and look what had happened.

"I didn't let him."

"You are a fucking idiot," Morgan snapped succinctly, and Nik shrugged. It wasn't like him to stand and take abuse from anybody, but somewhere in his messed up head, he had the overwhelming feeling Morgan was entitled to his anger. He would let Morgan say his piece and then they could move on. He could learn to stop being in love with this man. Morgan walked closer until maybe three feet separated them.

"I am sorry you were hurt. It was hard when you didn't wake up for four days," Nik said in his best professional voice. He didn't want to think about any of it; not the bullet, or Morgan's face, or the artificial coma that Morgan had been put into. "When they told me you had hit your head on the ground and you had bleeding on your brain—"

"It wasn't your fault, you know," Morgan interrupted. Nik wasn't ready to have Morgan dismiss things so easily.

"I should have been more vigilant. We knew there

was the very real chance that a price was still on your head."

Morgan crossed his arms across his chest. "You couldn't know for sure what Bullen had paid for."

"We don't know for sure it was Bullen."

"Bullshit, we know it's that slimy politician behind all this. I've done my research. I'm not stupid, you know. I can connect the dots as well as the next person. I want to find out why Elisabeth died, and I know the Bullen family was involved." Nik looked at the man standing in front of him, so strong and utterly certain, conviction in every bone of his body. "I hear you're moving into Ops for a while."

Jeez, Dale was clearly shit at keeping confidential information secret. "Just for the weeks I need to heal properly. Grunt work really. This—" He waved expansively. "—is my last assignment. I have to decommission this place before I get moved over."

"I know. It was my idea. We need to talk, and you wouldn't return my calls." *His idea?*

"I'm not doing this with you, Morgan. I got emotionally involved, and you got hurt. My eye was off the ball."

"You saw him. Jeez, you pushed yourself in front of him. What about that wasn't your job?"

"The part where the bullet didn't stop." This was just complete cruelty to have the only person he could ever love standing within reach and yet be so unobtainable. Morgan shook his head and then dropped his hands to his side, clenched into fists.

"Elisabeth has been forgotten in all of this. I want to

use your expertise to help me find what information she had and why she had to die because of it."

"So I can fuck that up, too?"

Something clearly snapped inside Morgan at the comment, and in two steps, he was there, in Nik's space, pulling his head down for a kiss. The simple taste of him was intoxicating to Nik. He didn't argue, and Morgan's tongue darted into his mouth, branding him with heat, enough to remind Nik what they'd had before. Angry and frustrated, he pushed Morgan away and took a long step back, wanting the space.

"What the fuck, Morgan?"

"Were you lying when you said you loved me? Was all of it a convenient lie?" Self-derision dripped from Morgan's words, and they immediately put Nik's back up.

"I don't lie." His emphatic response hung in the air between them and to see the fire in Morgan's eyes was to crave the thrill of a fight. Morgan moved quickly, back into his space, jabbing at his chest, his words sharp and angry and all kickass temper.

"You said you loved me; I said it back. Then through no fault of yours, I was hurt while you were doing your job. Why do you feel guilty? Because you didn't die? Because you only slowed the bullet? For some reason, you believe this negates any love we may have had. Am I right so far?"

"Morgan—"

Another jab of a finger, and Nik caught the hand in a tight grip. "Don't Morgan me, I will always want you, will always love you. I am so freaking happy the bullet went into my face. Do you know why?" His voice was full of passion.

"Shit. Don't say things like that."

"I'm happy because it meant it hadn't stayed in you. Do you understand that? What is wrong with you, Nik?"

Nik released the hold on Morgan's hand and stared openly at the new scar that puckered the flesh to the left and below Morgan's eye. "Your face," he started, completely unsure of how to tell this man what the scarring meant, how much of a reminder it was of what had gone wrong. Morgan inhaled sharply, and his face changed from anger and confusion to utter hurt.

"Okay, I... I get it. The scar is bad. I can't imagine wanting to look at it either." Then it was his turn to walk away, towards the cabin, the set of his shoulders square and tight.

"Morgan? What the hell? You idiot." Morgan didn't reply, and Nik followed him into the cool shady interior, squinting to see in the sudden change in lighting. He didn't see him in the front room and finally tracked him down to the small kitchen where he found him leaning over the sink, his hands braced on either side of the stainless steel basin. "Morgan?"

"I've kind of gotten used to it. I don't even notice it now, but I get that every time you see it, it would remind you."

Compassion ran through Nik. He was killing himself over this when all he wanted, all he needed, was standing next to him within touching distance. He placed a hand on Morgan's arm, the heat through his shirt a gentle reminder of his lover's warmth.

"How can you not blame me when all I can do is blame myself?"

"Because I am not some freaking idiot," Morgan snapped.

Could it be this easy? Was merely knowing Morgan didn't think he could have done anything else enough to let him forgive himself? Morgan tilted his head to face him, a wry smile on his face.

"I don't blame anyone, Nik, least of all you. You saved my life. And I say again, you are one huge fucking idiot. I don't fall in love on a whim. In fact, I have never been in love. For me this could well be my forever. I want it to be your forever, too." Nik's heart snapped wide open at those words. All the love, affection, and lust rose to the fore with a vengeance. Maybe Morgan was right. Maybe he could push past this idiotic bullshit that swirled in his head. Carefully Nik repositioned Morgan until his lover was against the wall, and he waited until Morgan's expression changed from shock to a smile. Nik gently traced the scar on his face with his lips, the texture strange to touch. He knew the puckered skin on his shoulder would feel similar. Morgan slid his hands up to circle Nik's neck. It was familiar and perfect.

"I love you, Morgan. I don't want anyone else. I'll work through the bullshit in my head. You'll just have to give me time."

"I'm still having dreams," Morgan said gently. "They only stopped in the cabin when I slept with you. I need more of that. I can help you; you can help me."

"So you want to team up and find out more about

Elisabeth?" Nik asked carefully, still waiting for the axe to fall.

"I do."

"I'm guessing Dale told you he is part of the team working on the Bullen case?" Nik had to get this out in the open; Morgan was too involved in all of this not to be briefed.

"He told me."

"They want him working the case officially."

"Did he decide what he was going to do?"

"I'm not sure. I stopped listening to him in the car." Nik didn't explain why and thankfully Morgan took it at face value. He tightened his grip on the back of Nik's head and drew him closer for a kiss. They stood that way for a long time, and then finally, Morgan pulled back.

"Did you know this place has a waterfall and a lake?" he asked with a devious smile.

"I remember from the plans," Nik replied, and then immediately knew where this was going and steeled himself for the begging.

"Hey, tough guy." Morgan grinned widely.

"What?"

"Wanna go swimming?"

THE END

The Sanctuary Series

The Bullen Arc

- Guarding Morgan (Book 1)
- The Only Easy Day (Book 2)
- Face Value (Book 3)
- Still Waters (Book 4)
- Full Circle (Book 5)
- The Journal Of Sanctuary One (Book 6)
- Worlds Collide (Book 7)

The Chicago Arc

- Accidental Hero (Book 8)
- Ghost (Book 9)
- By The Numbers (Book 10)

The Bullen Arc

Guarding Morgan (#1)

When Morgan's handler sends him to Nik for safety, neither Morgan nor Nik could imagine that two weeks alone in a cabin in the woods could start something more.

The Only Easy Day (#2)

Two SEALs both want the Bullen family brought to account,

but one wants justice and the other wants revenge

Face Value (#3)

When bullets start to fly there is only one thing between Beckett and death. Kayden.

Still Waters (#4)

Against the backdrop of Sanctuary and the Bullen case Adam and Lee realize not everything they saw was real.

Full Circle (#5)

When Manny risks his life could it finally be time for Josh to risk his heart?

Journal Of Sanctuary One (#6)

Neither man is prepared for being stuck together for an entire week, nor for the secrets that threaten to get them both killed

Worlds Collide (#7)

What no one factored in, not Sanctuary or the FBI, was the lengths Griffin Ryland would go to in the effort to protect himself.

————

The Chicago Arc

Accidental Hero (#8)

Chicago Cop Simon Grant and Sanctuary operative Cain Brodie, have to be the heroes of their own stories, just to stay alive.

Ghost (#9)

You can't hold onto a ghost, and sacrifice is often the only way to make things right.

By The Numbers (#10)

The only way of destroying Varga is to cut the crime boss's money, and the two men become part of an intricate take-down involving millions of dollars.

RJ Scott

RJ is the author of the over one hundred published novels and discovered romance in books at a very young age. She realized that if there wasn't romance on the page, she could create it in her head, and is a lifelong writer.

She lives and works out of her home in the beautiful English countryside, spends her spare time reading, watching films, and enjoying time with her family.

The last time she had a week's break from writing she didn't like it one little bit and has yet to meet a bottle of wine she couldn't defeat.

www.rjscott.co.uk | rj@rjscott.co.uk

facebook.com/author.rjscott

twitter.com/Rjscott_author

instagram.com/rjscott_author

bookbub.com/authors/rj-scott

pinterest.com/rjscottauthor

Printed in Great Britain
by Amazon